"I need to get upstairs and take a shower."

"Yeah, I need to do the same," Daniel replied.

"We could always shower together and save water."

She had to be joking, Daniel thought. But as he turned and looked at Lizzie there was no teasing light in her eyes. It stole his breath away.

She took a step closer to him, her whiskey eyes inviting him to imbibe, to become intoxicated with her. "I didn't tell you about one of the things on my bucket list."

"And what's that?" he asked, aware that his voice sounded half-strangled with his need of her.

"To make love to a man I'll never forget. I believe that you're that man, Daniel. I want to make love to you, and when I leave here I'll have the warmth of that memory of us together to carry with me for the rest of my life."

Dear Reader,

I can't think of anything more distracting that a hot and sexy cowboy with a hint of darkness in his eyes. In *Her Cowboy Distraction,* my hero, Daniel Jefferson, is that man.

There's something enduring and solid about a cowboy, and I love writing cowboy heroes. This is the first book of a series that centers around a café in the small town of Grady Gulch, Oklahoma.

Daniel Jefferson has suffered enormous tragedy in his life and has no desire to ever reach out for love again. Lizzy Wiles is a woman on a mission and isn't ready for a relationship with any man. But when she breezes into the Cowboy Café to take a waitressing job and becomes the target for a killer, her world collides with Daniel's in a way neither of them could have expected.

I hope you enjoy reading *Her Cowboy Distraction* as much as I enjoyed writing it.

As always, thanks for your support.

Happy reading!

Carla Cassidy

CARLA CASSIDY

Her Cowboy Distraction

ROMANTIC
SUSPENSE

Recycling programs
for this product may
not exist in your area.

ISBN-13: 978-0-373-27781-0

HER COWBOY DISTRACTION

www.Harlequin.com

Printed in U.S.A.

Books by Carla Cassidy

Harlequin Romantic Suspense

Rancher Under Cover #1676
Cowboy's Triplet Trouble #1681
Tool Belt Defender #1687
Mercenary's Perfect Mission #1708
**Her Cowboy Distraction* #1711

Silhouette Romantic Suspense

†*Man on a Mission* #1077
Born of Passion #1094
†*Once Forbidden…* #1115
†*To Wed and Protect* #1126
†*Out of Exile* #1149
Secrets of a Pregnant Princess #1166
††*Last Seen…* #1233
††*Dead Certain* #1250
††*Trace Evidence* #1261
††*Manhunt* #1294
‡*Protecting the Princess* #1345
‡*Defending the Rancher's Daughter* #1376
‡*The Bodyguard's Promise* #1419
‡*The Bodyguard's Return* #1447
‡*Safety in Numbers* #1463
‡*Snowbound with the Bodyguard* #1521
‡*Natural-Born Protector* #1527

A Hero of Her Own #1548
‡*The Rancher Bodyguard* #1551
5 Minutes to Marriage #1576
The Cowboy's Secret Twins #1584
His Case, Her Baby #1600
The Lawman's Nanny Op #1615
Cowboy Deputy #1639
Special Agent's Surrender #1648

†The Delaney Heirs
††Cherokee Corners
‡Wild West Bodyguards
*Lawmen of Black Rock
**Cowboy Café

Other titles by this author available
   in ebook format.

CARLA CASSIDY

is an award–winning author who has written more than one hundred books for Harlequin Books. In 1995 she won Best Silhouette Romance from *RT Book Reviews* for *Anything for Danny*. In 1998 she also won a Career Achievement Award for Best Innovative Series from *RT Book Reviews*.

Carla believes the only thing better than curling up with a good book to read is sitting down at the computer with a good story to write. She's looking forward to writing many more books and bringing hours of pleasure to readers.

Chapter 1

Lizzy Wiles blew a strand of her long brown hair away from the side of her face as she poured George Wilton another cup of coffee. "How's that meat loaf?" she asked the old man, who seemed to wear a perpetual frown every time he came into the café. She already knew what the answer would be because they had had this same conversation every Friday night for the past month since Lizzy had started working as a waitress at the Cowboy Café.

"Dry. The meat loaf is always dry," George grumbled.

"George, every Friday night the special is meat loaf, and every Friday night you come in here and order the special. Why don't you try something else if you don't like the meat loaf?"

George's grizzled gray eyebrows pulled together

across his forehead. "But, I like Mary's meat loaf. It's just dry. Why would I want to order anything else?"

"Just asking," Lizzy replied with a wry smile as she turned to put the coffeepot back on the burner. She grabbed a clean wet towel to wipe up one area of the long counter and gave a quick glance at her wristwatch.

Quarter to seven. On Friday and Saturday nights the café stayed open until midnight. For the rest of the five days a week the usual closing time was ten o'clock.

Lizzy came in at two in the afternoons and closed six days a week. She'd blown into the small town of Grady Gulch, Oklahoma, a month ago and had decided that the Cowboy Café was the perfect place to accomplish two of the items on her bucket list at the same time: meet a cowboy and work as a waitress in a small café.

Mary Mathis, the pretty owner of the café, had taken Lizzy under her wing, not only giving her a job but also a place to stay in one of the four small cabins directly behind the restaurant.

As she wiped the counter she glanced around the café. The dinner crowd had finally thinned out, and for the first time she felt as if she could take a deep breath and slow down the crazy pace she kept up from four to about six-thirty each evening.

She checked her watch once again. Five minutes and he'd walk through the door. Every Friday night that she'd worked there he'd always arrived at precisely seven o'clock.

He always sat in the same place, the third booth next to the window. Lizzy worked the counter, never the booths. She'd asked Candy Bailey, the waitress who worked the booth section of the restaurant, what she knew about the lone cowboy, but Candy had been working at the café only a few weeks longer than Lizzy and didn't know anything about him.

Not that Lizzy really wanted to know any intimate details about him. It was just idle curiosity, that's all. He was hot and handsome and always alone. It was just interesting. Still, at seven o'clock when the little bell over the door tinkled and he walked in, Lizzy's heartbeat quickened more than just a little bit.

He was a tall drink of water clad in a worn pair of jeans, which hugged his slender hips and long legs, and a white T-shirt that stretched taut across his broad shoulders.

The first thing he did after entering the front door was remove the black cowboy hat from his head and hang it on one of the many hooks that were screwed into the wall by the door.

Mary Mathis had a rule in her establishment: no hats allowed while eating. She'd made it easy with the hooks for the cowboys coming in to abide by her strict rule.

Mr. Hot Cowboy's slightly unruly dark hair showed no residual effect from having worn the hat. His hair held just enough lazy curl to make a woman want to run her hands through it. Not that Lizzy would ever consider doing that. It was just something she'd noticed.

She rewashed the counter area she'd just cleaned as she surreptitiously watched him walk to the third booth, which had last held a rather unruly family of four.

He sat, as he always did, on the side of the booth facing the door. He never picked up a menu, and he rarely greeted anyone else who might be in the café at the same time.

He was like an island unto himself, sculptured features set in granite as he stared at the laminated tabletop as if it might hold all of the answers to life's mysteries.

There was no question that he pulled a sharp physical response from Lizzy. She'd been in town for a little over a month, and she definitely thought he was the hottest thing walking in the small town of Grady Gulch.

"Lizzy, order up," Mary's pleasant voice called from the pass window.

Lizzy turned away from the eye candy and hurried to the window that separated the dining area and the kitchen. "Tell Fred that the steak is grilled just the way he likes it, still half mooing on the plate," Mary said. "And you can take a break if you want to. Things have slowed down since the dinner rush has passed."

"Thanks, Mary." Lizzy picked up the platter that held a rare steak, an oversize baked potato and green beans. She walked down to the end of the counter where Fred Jenkins, who worked as the town's only vet, sat on the end stool.

"Mary said it's still mooing, so you should be happy," she said with a smile at the balding middle-aged man as she placed the platter in front of him.

"That's the way I like it, either rare on the plate or healthy on the hoof," he replied. "Hey, by the way, I've got a litter of schnauzer pups I'm trying to find homes for. You interested in a puppy?"

"No thanks," she replied quickly, although her mind instantly filled with the vision of adorable button brown eyes and sweet puppy kisses. "I love dogs, but my life-style just isn't conducive to me having one. Footloose and fancy-free, that's me. But, if you'd like, I'll ask around for you."

"That would be great," Fred replied.

"Anything else I can get for you? I'm going on break."

"Nope, I'm good," he said. "Enjoy your break."

A few minutes later Lizzy sat at a table near the counter with a cup of freshly brewed coffee before her. There was a small break room in the back, but Lizzy rarely took her breaks there. She preferred to sit here at the small table in the dining area and people watch... especially on Friday nights when *he* came in.

She took a sip from her cup and glanced in his direction. Candy was in the process of delivering his order. He always ordered the same thing, two pieces of peach pie and one cup of coffee.

As Candy left the booth he pulled one of the slices of pie in front of him and shoved the other to the opposite side, as if anticipating the arrival of another diner. But, in the four weeks that Lizzy had watched this ritual, no other diner had ever shown up to sit across from him.

He'd eat his pie, drink his coffee and not make eye contact with anyone in the place. Then he'd leave and the second piece of untouched pie would be thrown in the trash. It was a waste of good pie, but more than that it seemed like such a waste of good man.

Lizzy had speculated for the past four weeks each time he'd been in the café. All she could figure out was that each week he made a date with somebody he hoped would show up but who never did. Although

Lizzy couldn't imagine a man like him being stood up by any woman with a beating heart.

Suddenly she wanted to make some kind of contact with him. She'd thought about him often after the first Friday night she'd seen him and had watched his actions and that spare piece of pie bite the dust.

You wouldn't dare, a little voice whispered in the back of her head as an idea began to form. *It would be completely rude, wouldn't it? He'd think you were completely crazy.* She tried to talk herself out of the strong impulse that had sprung into her mind.

But, she would dare. Since her mother's death four months before, Lizzy was doing a lot of things she would have never considered doing before.

She hadn't even realized she'd made up her mind to follow through on her impulse when she found herself on her feet, her coffee cup in hand as she headed for the third booth from the window and the handsome cowboy who sat all alone.

She didn't give herself a chance to think, to second-guess what she was doing as she slid into the booth seat across from him and set her coffee cup on the table next to the extra piece of peach pie.

Gray eyes. She hadn't been close enough to him until now to see the color of his eyes. His stunning, long-lashed gray eyes stared at her as if she were a creature from another planet.

She gave him one of her brightest smiles. "As you can see from my name tag, my name is Lizzy Wiles. Well, actually my name is Elizabeth Wiles, but everyone has always called me Lizzy."

She noticed he'd already eaten half his slice of pie, and he continued to stare at her as she picked up the spare fork and took a bite of the piece of pie in front of her. "It seems such a shame to throw this away after you leave each week. Personally, my favorite is apple, but Mary makes a mean pie no matter what kind it is."

Up close he was nothing short of amazing. Chiseled cheekbones and a firm square jaw radiated masculine strength, but his full lower lip whispered of something hot and dangerously sexy.

Still, it was his eyes that captured and held her. They were shadowed pools that, at the moment, simmered not only with a vague astonishment, but also with an underlying sadness that she hadn't expected, that seemed to pierce through her very soul.

"So, what's your name, cowboy?" she asked, aware that she sounded like a heroine in a Western romance novel.

The fork he held in his hand had never wavered until now. He carefully set it down next to his half-eaten pie, his eyes still holding that look of ambiguous surprise.

Before she realized his intention, he slid out of the booth, walked to the front door, grabbed his hat and then disappeared out of the café.

She stared after him, horrified that she'd apparently offended a paying customer to the point he'd left the café. He hadn't even finished his pie.

Her heart thundering with the feeling that she'd just made a dreadful mistake, she got up from the booth. *What have you done, Lizzy? You should have just taken your break and minded your own darned business,* a little voice inside her head chided.

She hurried into the kitchen, where she found Mary, the owner of the café, seated on a stool at a small table while Junior Lempke worked the grill, his tree-trunk-sized arms bulging beneath a grease-stained T-shirt.

"Mary, I think I just did something awful," Lizzy said as she pulled up a stool next to her boss. Lizzy's heart still banged painfully fast as she looked at Mary.

Mary Mathis was an attractive blonde with soft blue eyes and a beautiful smile. She not only mothered her ten-year-old son, Matt, but also her entire staff. "Lizzy, I've only known you a month, but I can't imagine you ever doing something awful," she replied.

Lizzy's cheeks burned with sudden shame. She should have never listened to that evil inner voice of hers. "You know that guy who comes in every Friday night and sits all by himself and orders two pieces of peach pie and a cup of coffee?"

Mary nodded. "Daniel Jefferson."

Daniel Jefferson. Lizzy now had a name to go with the handsome face and the hot body. "I ate his peach pie," Lizzy blurted out. "The extra piece, I mean. It was just a crazy impulse," she added hurriedly. "I'd watched him every Friday night and nobody ever joined him to eat the pie, so tonight I decided to."

Mary's blue eyes widened with surprise. "Oh, my goodness. What on earth did he do?"

"Nothing. He never said a word to me. He just got up and left the café."

Mary took a sip of her iced tea and gazed at Junior,

who was carefully flipping a burger, a frown of deep concentration across his broad forehead. "Maybe it's a good thing." She looked back at Lizzy. "Maybe you shook him up just a little bit. Lord knows that man needs something other than his grief to think about."

"Grief?"

Mary nodded. "Daniel and his wife, Janice, used to come in here every Friday night for pie and coffee."

Wife. Of course a man who looked like Daniel Jefferson would have a wife. She frowned at Mary. "But, if he has a wife, then why since I've been working here does he always come in all alone?"

"About a year and a half ago Janice and her best friend, Cherry Benson, were killed in a car accident. It was a terrible tragedy, both for Daniel and the Benson men, who had already lost their parents years ago. Anyway, every Friday night since Janice's death Daniel has continued what had been their tradition of coming in for pie and coffee."

"And the pie I ate was meant for his dead wife." Lizzy swallowed hard against her horror. She felt as if she'd somehow spit on his wife's grave. "Oh, I feel so awful. I'm so stupid."

"You aren't stupid," Mary replied. "You just didn't know his background."

"What should I do now? How can I make this right?"

Lizzy thought of the sadness she'd seen in his eyes. Grief. It was definitely an emotion Lizzy understood intimately, still suffered from when it came to her mother's recent death.

"You should do nothing." Mary got up from her stool

and offered Lizzy a sweet smile. "Stop looking so worried. Daniel is a big boy and you might want to apologize to him when he comes in here again, but other than that don't give it another minute of thought."

Easy for her to say, Lizzy thought that night at closing time. She'd been able to think of nothing but Daniel Jefferson for the rest of the evening as she'd worked.

He'd lost his wife. What a tragedy and it was obvious he'd loved her desperately, had shared with her that forever kind of love that Lizzy had only read about. Almost two years was a long time to grieve, a long time to keep alive a tradition that kept his dead wife in the forefront of his mind.

Daniel Jefferson was off-limits for any number of reasons, despite the fact that just looking at him made her feel a little breathless. Lizzy wasn't looking for love. She was looking for adventure, fulfilling a promise she'd made to her dying mother, a promise that would have her leaving Grady Gulch in the next couple of weeks to continue her journey of adventure.

Even if she was going to stick around for a while, the worst thing she could do was indulge in some kind of crazy crush on a man who was caught up in grief, clinging to a love that could probably never be replaced. That would be just plain stupid, and Lizzy didn't do stupid.

After closing up the café, Lizzy and two other young women who had worked that night left the building, walking together to the small cabins they were temporarily calling home.

Candy stayed in the one on the left of Lizzy's and Courtney Chambers with her ten-month-old son lived in the cabin on Lizzy's right. The fourth cabin was occupied by Rusty Albright, a forty-something man who worked as a cook/manager when Mary wasn't working the kitchen.

Candy was twenty-three years old, five years younger than Lizzy and, according to what she'd told Lizzy, had moved from a nearby small town into the cabin to work for Mary and be closer to her boyfriend, who was a Grady Gulch native.

Courtney had been taken in by Mary when at twenty-four years old she'd found herself pregnant and alone and disowned by her parents. She never spoke about the father of her little boy, but Lizzy knew he wasn't part of Courtney's life and didn't contribute to her financially.

"My feet and my back are killing me," Candy said plaintively as they walked. It was a complaint she voiced every night. In the brief time Lizzy had known her, she'd realized Candy complained about everything. "I wish I could afford a massage, but on the tips I make here I'll never be able to afford anything."

"Actually, my tips are always pretty good," Lizzy replied, wishing she had the nerve to tell Candy that a positive attitude was a good thing to possess in life.

"I just want to go pick up Garrett from the babysitter and then get a good night's sleep," Courtney said. "I'm off tomorrow, so I'll be able to spend the whole day with my baby boy." Courtney's face shone with her love for her son.

"Yuck. No offense, but I can't think of a worse way to spend a day off," Candy exclaimed. "I don't want to think about babies for a long time."

"Are you planning anything special with little Garrett?" Lizzy asked.

"No, just a day of Mommy and Garrett time," Courtney replied. "He'll be happy if I give him an empty box to play with."

Candy released a dramatic sigh. "I'm just hoping Kevin wants to do something fun tomorrow besides hang out with his friends, drink and argue." She sighed again. "That's all we seem to be doing lately when we're together."

By this time the three had reached the point where they each went their separate ways. "Good night, ladies. Enjoy your day off and think about me while you're both having fun." Lizzy gave a small wave to the two of them and then headed to the door of her cabin.

Inside, a small lamp illuminated the area around the sofa sleeper that was already pulled out to make a bed. Lizzy never left to go to work in the afternoon without leaving a light on to greet her when she returned.

If you counted the bathroom, the cabins were two rooms, with the sofa bed providing the sleeping area, and a kitchenette that was little more than a sink, a small fridge and a microwave.

The rent Mary charged on these small units was next to nothing when she rented them to the waitresses who worked at the restaurant.

Lizzy went directly into the tiny bathroom and stripped off the jeans and Cowboy Café T-shirt that was the uniform for the waitresses. She tossed the clothes in a hamper and then stepped into the shower, wanting the feel of grease and grime of work off her skin before getting into bed.

The minute she stepped beneath the warm spray of water her mind filled with a vision of *him*. Daniel Jefferson. He definitely wasn't a Danny, not with those stone-hard features and dark gray eyes. The name *Danny* implied somebody fun-loving and happy. There had been nothing happy about Daniel.

The couple of bites of peach pie she'd eaten had been sweet and delicious going down, but they had become tart and terrible when Mary had told her Daniel's story. She'd eaten the pie he'd apparently meant as some sort of tribute to his dead wife. Jeez, could she have done anything worse?

Although the last thing Lizzy was looking for in her life was love, she couldn't help but wonder what it would be like to be loved that deeply.

She threw her head beneath the warm spray of water, hoping it would wash away some of her feelings of guilt and any other thoughts of Daniel Jefferson.

Mary Mathis awoke suddenly, her heart pounding violently. Couldn't breathe. Her lungs squeezed tight and ached with the need to draw air. She sat up and managed a gasp.

You're safe. Nobody can harm you. Just breathe. The rational little whisper in the back of her brain slowly calmed her. *Just breathe.*

Her heartbeat finally slowed to a more normal pace and she sat for several moments and drew in deep breaths to steady herself.

From the faint illumination of the night-light plugged into the wall next to the bed she could see that nothing was amiss in the small room, that all was as it had been when she'd gone to sleep.

There were no strange noises, nothing to be afraid of. She was safe here, and the terror of whatever dream she'd suffered slowly fell away.

She knew from experience that any further sleep would be impossible for a while. She never went directly back to sleep after one of these awakening panic episodes.

Always the first thing she did after waking in the middle of the night was get out of bed and walk across the living room to the bedroom where her ten-year-old son slept.

She now stood in the doorway of the larger second bedroom, her heart filled with love as she gazed at the towheaded boy who sprawled in the bed as if frozen in the middle of motion.

That was Matt, always moving, always smiling. He was a happy boy who loved his mother and loved this place they had called home for the past eight years.

He was the glue that held her together on nights like this, when panic swelled up inside her and unwanted terrible memories tumbled through her mind.

He was such a good kid. He did well in school, had a kind heart and lots of friends in this small town that had embraced them when they'd arrived here.

She moved away from his door and went back into the living room. She turned on one of the lamps next to the sofa and sank into its overstuffed comfort.

The apartment consisting of two bedrooms, a living room and a large bathroom was located in the back of the café. According to Violet Grady, the old woman Mary had bought the place from, her father had had only enough money to build one building, so he'd decided to put the café and his living quarters all under one roof. The only thing that separated the living space from the business was a locked door in the café kitchen.

Mary loved the fact that when she was at work Matt was only a few steps away at home. She could be a responsible business owner and a present mother at the same time.

Who would have ever thought that at thirty-three years old she'd live in a small town like Grady Gulch, own the Cowboy Café and be happy feeding the townspeople and watching her son thrive and grow?

Sometimes it scared her when she looked back on the past eight years and realized that for the most part fate had been responsible for her good fortune and the place she was at in her life now. She'd worked as a waitress for three years in the café before Violet had come to her with a plan to help Mary buy the place. Violet had been like an angel sent to Mary when Mary had lost all hope.

But, Mary never forgot where she'd come from, the horrible events that had eventually led her to be here and now. She never forgot that in the blink of fate's capricious eye it could all be destroyed.

That's what made her sometimes sit up in the middle of the night with her heart pounding and in the grip of a panic attack, because she knew her business, her happiness and her son could all be taken away from her. And the worst part was that there were times when she believed that might be what she deserved.

Chapter 2

Daniel stood on the back deck of his house, still half reeling with shock at the waitress's actions in the café even though he'd left there hours before.

It was as if he'd just been jerked awake from a lifetime nap and was more than a little surprised to find himself still breathing.

He'd been in a fog and suddenly it had lifted and there was a strange woman seated across from him, a woman with long brown hair with shiny blond highlights, an impudent upturned nose and eyes the color of whiskey. Her smile had been so wonderfully warm as she'd eaten the pie he'd ordered for the wife he'd lost.

As always, thoughts of Janice brought with them a crushing guilt that pressed so tightly against his chest it left him almost breathless.

For the first time in almost two years he consciously

shoved away those thoughts and instead brought a picture of the waitress from the café into his mind.

Lizzy.

Elizabeth Wiles, but everyone called her Lizzy. She definitely wasn't from Grady Gulch. He'd lived there all his life and knew practically everyone in town. Besides, nobody who was a Grady Gulch native would have had the gumption to do what she had done.

For the most part for the past eighteen months, everyone in town had pretty much left him alone in his prolonged grief and guilt stupor.

He hadn't noticed her in the café before tonight, but that didn't mean anything. Daniel had stopped looking at people, had stopped taking in his surroundings when he left his ranch, since the day he'd buried Janice.

In the cast of the moonlight overhead he could see his cattle in the distance, some of them lying down for sleep, others grazing on the early summer grass. He turned his gaze upward.

Here in the country the stars looked close enough to grasp in your hands. Her eyes had held a sparkle like the stars. Lizzy's eyes.

What had stunned him more than anything was that for just a moment as he'd stared at her, as he'd seen that spark in her eyes and the warmth of her smile, an unexpected surge of energy, of life had washed through him. It was something he hadn't felt for a very long time.

With a deep sigh he turned and went back into the big house that resonated with a depth of silence he'd almost become accustomed to experiencing each time he walked through the door. Almost.

He needed to go to bed. It was just past midnight and there would be chores to get done early in the morning. But, he'd always found sleep difficult on Friday nights, when thoughts of Janice intruded heavily into his head.

Still, as he got into bed minutes later, it wasn't thoughts of Janice that filled his head, but rather thoughts of Lizzy, who preferred apple to peach and had, for just a minute, made Daniel feel something other than his own pain.

He fell asleep with a vision of whiskey-colored eyes in his head and awakened just after dawn with the same emptiness that had been his life for the past year and a half.

This ranch was where he'd been raised, the only child of a couple who'd had him in their mid-forties. They'd built the large house with the expectation of filling it with lots of children. Unfortunately, the children hadn't happened until Daniel, and there were no more after him.

His parents hadn't lived long enough to see him married, and thankfully they hadn't been alive to see him widowed. There were times he wished he had a brother or a sister, somebody who would help him get through this endless grief process, and at other times he felt he deserved to never stop the sadness that filled his very soul.

If things had been different, he would have turned to his best friend, Sam Benson, or one of Sam's brothers. But Sam's sister had died in the accident that had also killed Janice. The friendship that Daniel had shared with Sam and his younger brothers had been strained ever since.

The week passed quickly, as each one always did, with his mind emptied except for the daily chores that were involved in running a ranch with cattle, horses, a coop full of chickens and crops.

Each day unfolded like the last one, with Daniel spending as much time as possible outside and going into the big, silent house only to shower, eat and sleep.

It was on Friday evening after dinner as he showered for his regular trip into town that he thought again of the waitress at the Cowboy Café.

The ritual of driving into town each Friday night, of sitting in the café and ordering the pie he and Janice used to eat every Friday night of their courtship and marriage, had been part of his penance.

Since her death, each week when he showered to prepare for the night, he'd always been filled with a sense of dread, with the wish that he could turn back time and somehow make things different. But, of course, that was impossible. There was no going back in time to fix things. Some things simply couldn't be fixed.

Now as he stood beneath the hot spray of water he felt something much different, and he knew it had to do with the waitress. Lizzy, who had slid into the booth seat across from him and eaten his dead wife's pie, had also managed to shake him out of his numb state enough to fill him with a strange sizzle of anticipation as he thought of encountering her once again.

It was six-forty when he left the house for the fifteen-minute drive into town to the café. He kept his driver's-side window down, allowing in the sweet scents of early summer that emanated from the pastures and fields he passed.

Funny, he hadn't noticed the smells of home for a long time. All he'd been able to smell was the scent of his own misery, the odor of his remorse.

A knot of tension formed in his chest, a knot that tightened the closer he got to the café. This time he recognized that the tension had nothing to do with his past, but rather was an anticipation of the night to come.

Would Lizzy be working tonight? He'd been too shocked by her actions to utter a single word to her the week before. He had no idea what her normal hours were at the café. If she was there tonight he wasn't sure he would speak to her, but the fact that he was even considering it came as a complete surprise to him.

It was just a few minutes before seven when he parked his truck in front of the café. He sat for several moments, gripping the steering wheel as he stared at the ancient establishment.

The Cowboy Café had been around forever. Housed in a low, flat red building, a billboard on the roof boasted a cowboy wearing a hat to announce its presence in the area.

The café was *the* place in town for good food, a warm, inviting atmosphere and all the local gossip you could want. Mary Mathis updated the menus occasionally, but for the most part the café had remained pretty much the same over the years. The place was essentially the very heart of Grady Gulch.

He got out of his truck, and as he walked toward the

door his emotions suddenly felt wildly out of control. He shouldn't be thinking about a waitress with amber-colored eyes and silky brown hair. He shouldn't be remembering the warmth of her smile, the vibrancy of her very presence opposite him in the booth.

He should be focused solely on the blond-haired, blue-eyed woman who had been his wife, a woman whose death, and that of her best friend, rested solely on his head.

Still, the minute the bell over the door tinkled to announce his arrival and he stepped into the air that smelled of savory scents, that rang with the boisterous noise of people dining and laughing, his gaze shot around the room.

Instantly his gaze locked with hers.

Lizzy.

She stood behind the counter, but it was as if she hadn't been working at all but rather had been just standing there watching the door, waiting for him to arrive.

In an instant he took in everything about her, the way her shiny hair had half escaped a low ponytail, how her T-shirt fit snug across her breasts and molded to her slender waist.

In that frozen moment of eye contact he noted the slight widening of her eyes, the way her lips parted as if on a gasp, and a crackling tension snapped in the air.

He wasn't sure who looked away first, he or she. He hung up his hat and then made his way to his usual booth and told himself that he was there to honor his dead wife, to punish himself for all the things he'd done wrong on the last night of her life.

He definitely wasn't there with any other purpose in mind other than the somber ritual that he felt compelled to perform. He slid into the booth, consciously keeping his gaze away from the counter area and Lizzy.

It didn't take long for Candy, the young woman who usually waited on him, to appear at the side of his booth. "The usual?" she asked, as she did every Friday night.

"Yeah," he replied. "No, wait," he added before she could move away from the booth. He drew a deep breath and wondered if he'd completely lost his mind. "Make that a piece of peach pie and a piece of apple."

Lizzy had been on edge all afternoon, wondering if Daniel would show up this evening. She'd imagined herself apologizing to him in a million different ways throughout the day. The minute he'd walked through the door her anxiety had shot through the ceiling.

She definitely owed him an apology. All week long she'd thought about it, thought about him, and hoped he'd show up tonight so she could apologize to him and assuage at least some of her guilt about what she had done.

Now he was there and yet she stood in place, nervous butterflies whirling around in the pit of her stomach. For just a moment as he'd walked in the door he'd made eye contact with her, and a flush of heat had washed over her. She didn't know if it was embarrassment that she felt or something else altogether. She'd whirled around and busied herself filling a napkin holder.

When she'd looked again Candy was serving him the usual, a cup of coffee and two slices of pie. When the waitress moved away from the booth once again, Lizzy sucked in a deep breath for courage and finally approached his booth.

She stopped a foot away from where he sat. "Mr. Jefferson?"

He turned to look at her with those dark gray eyes of his, and the butterflies in her tummy zoomed around at warp speed. "Uh…I just wanted to say how sorry I am for…uh…what I did, you know, last week…sitting down and…"

He held up a hand to halt her stuttering, awkward apology. "It's apple." He nodded his head to indicate the pie on the opposite side of the booth. "You told me you preferred apple."

Lizzy stared at him in surprise and then looked down at the piece of Mary's apple pie that he apparently meant for her to sit down and eat.

She'd thought he might yell at her. She believed it possible he might completely ignore her, but nothing like this scenario had ever entered her mind.

She glanced at the counter. There were only two diners seated there, and it was usually about this time in the evening that Mary told her she could take a break.

She slid into the seat across from him, feeling as if she were having a slight out-of-body experience. She wasn't even sure what to say to him.

"Apology accepted," he said. He had a nice voice, deep and smooth. He gazed at her with an intensity that simmered inside her. "You aren't from around here."

"No, I'm not." The shock was beginning to wear off enough to at least allow her to speak.

"So, tell me, Elizabeth, but everyone calls you Lizzy, how you wound up sitting across from me and eating my pie here in Grady Gulch." He cupped his big hands around his cup of coffee and looked at her with curiosity.

Lizzy picked up her fork and cut through the pie, the cinnamon-apple scent instantly reminding her of her mother's house. Her mother had always loved to bake. "I'm originally from Chicago. Four months ago my mother passed away, but before she died she made me promise that I'd get to my bucket list right away."

"'Bucket list'?" He frowned in obvious puzzlement.

"You know, a list of all the things you want to do before you kick the bucket...before you die."

"Your mother was worried about you dying soon?" His frown deepened, tugging his dark eyebrows closer together.

"No, not at all," Lizzy replied hurriedly. "Although I think she was afraid I was going to work myself into an early grave. At the time I was working in an ad agency. Brutal hours, no time for fun or downtime. I was in the fast lane for success, and I think Mom worried that I'd forgotten what was really important in life."

Lizzy paused a moment and took a bite of the pie, thankful when he broke eye contact for a moment to pick up his fork. She was aware that she was talking too much, too fast, but seemed unable to stop herself.

"Anyway," she continued, "Mom had a bucket list of all the things she'd planned to do when she retired, when she had the time and the money to explore and have adventures." A rush of emotion rose up, but Lizzy swallowed it back with another bite of pie. "Unfortunately she hadn't planned on cancer. Two days before she passed she made me promise to take my inheritance and fulfill my bucket list now rather than waiting until I was older and settled. So, that's what I'm doing in her honor."

"And one of the things on your bucket list was to be a waitress in Grady Gulch?" He looked at her as if she might just be a little bit crazy.

She grinned. "No, not specifically, although waitressing in a small café was one of the things on my list, along with selling surfboards on a beach in California and working in a gift shop in the Grand Canyon. I've already done both those things. I was driving across the country when I stumbled onto Grady Gulch and the Cowboy Café and decided this would be my next stop."

"Stumbling across Grady Gulch is about the only way you'd find it," he said wryly as he cut through his piece of pie. "It's kind of a strange bucket list." Once again his gray eyes sought hers. "Most people would have skydiving, or a worldwide cruise or visiting a foreign country on their list."

She nodded. "I know, but I wanted to explore the United States rather than a foreign country," she explained. "And what I wanted to do was take jobs for short periods of time in different areas of the country that put me in touch with a variety of people. Meeting a cowboy was on my list, and I managed to accomplish that here, too."

Just a whisper of a smile curved his lips, and the

result of that small gesture shot a burst of surprising warmth through Lizzy. "You can't take a step in this town without crunching the brim of some cowboy's hat," he said. "So, have you finished your bucket list?"

"Oh no, I've really only just gotten started. I'll probably be here for another couple of weeks or so, and then I'll be moving on."

"Moving on to where? What else is on this list of yours?"

Lizzy looked over at the counter, making sure that none of her customers was trying to get her attention. Everyone seemed satisfied, so she took another bite of the apple pie and then answered him.

"Stargazing from a mountaintop. Singing on a corner in Times Square. Learn to ride a horse. Take some kind of dance lessons."

She ticked off part of her list, but consciously didn't tell him that one of the things on it was to make love to a man she'd never forget. She knew it was corny and ridiculously romantic and she hadn't actually written it down on paper, but it was on the bucket list in her head.

"I could help you with one of those things," he said.

A rivulet of shock jerked through her, and for a moment she wondered if he'd heard her thoughts. "What?" her voice squeaked in surprise.

"I've some nice saddle horses. I could teach you to ride."

She blinked as his words penetrated into her brain. Ride a horse, that's what he was talking about. Of course that's what he was talking about.

Certainly a man who loved his wife so deeply that

almost two years after her death he still had shadows of grief in his eyes, a man who still ordered his dead wife a piece of pie, wouldn't be volunteering to be the passionate lover she'd never forget.

"That would be great," she exclaimed, surprised by his offer. "I've always wanted to ride a horse, but I've never even been up close to one before."

"When do you have a day off?"

"Monday. I'm off all day and night." She tried to tamp down the stutter of her accelerated heartbeat.

"Where are you staying?"

"In one of the cabins out back."

He looked down at his coffee cup for a long moment and then met her gaze once again. It was impossible to read him through his eyes, which remained dark and enigmatic.

"Why don't I pick you up around nine on Monday morning. We'll go out to my place and you can meet my horses and we'll plan a little trail ride."

A rush of anticipation swept through her, and she wasn't sure if it was a result of knowing she'd accomplish something from her bucket list or if it was because that meant she would be spending more time with him.

Something about Daniel Jefferson intrigued her. Something about him excited her, and that wasn't necessarily a good thing. One of her personal rules was to never get too close to anyone in her travels. She had people to meet and places to see before she finally settled down to begin real life again, and she was determined to fulfill the promise she'd made to her mother—to complete her bucket list.

"That would be great," she heard herself reply.

There was a moment of awkward silence as he took another bite of his pie and gazed down at the tabletop. At that moment, Lizzy glanced back to the counter and saw that one of her diners was holding up his coffee cup toward her, indicating he needed a refill.

"I've got to get back to work," she said. "Thanks for the apology acceptance and the pie." She slid out of the booth. "I'll see you Monday morning."

She was conscious of his gaze following her as she left the booth and hurried back to the counter. She refilled coffee cups, got a bottle of ketchup for Mr. Criswell's fries, and when she looked back at the booth Daniel was gone.

A sigh of wonder whooshed out of her at the same time Mary sidled up next to her. "Okay, spill the beans. I saw you sitting at his booth for a few minutes. What happened?" she asked.

"He accepted my apology and he ordered me a piece of your apple pie," Lizzy replied. "And he's picking me up Monday morning to take me to his place to meet his horses and teach me how to ride." She still couldn't quite believe what had just happened.

She frowned and looked at Mary. "You're not going to tell me he's really some kind of a creep, are you?"

"No, on the contrary, he's a very nice man." Mary narrowed her eyes and gazed at Lizzy speculatively. "He's been through a really rough time." She hesitated a moment and then continued. "Please don't break his heart, Lizzy."

She looked at her boss in surprise. "That's the very

last thing I intend to do. I'm not interested in that kind of a relationship with him or anyone else, and besides, it's obvious he's still in mourning for his wife. It was just a piece of pie, Mary."

Mary nodded. "And really none of my business," she said. "I just know he's already had enough hurt to last an entire lifetime."

"And the last thing I want to do is inflict any more in his life," Lizzy replied. Besides, Daniel wasn't in a place to want anything from her romantically, and she didn't intend to be in town long enough for anything like that to happen.

All she was looking for was a little time on a horse and some pleasant conversation. No man, no matter how sexy, no matter how nice, was going to detour her from the path she'd chosen to follow.

Chapter 3

Daniel had no idea what had possessed him to offer Lizzy riding lessons. Monday morning as he led several of his most gentle saddle horses into the small corral next to the barn, he decided it was simply because she had managed to do what no other person in the entire town had been able to do: she'd penetrated through the veil of darkness he'd cloaked around himself enough to intrigue him.

And she did intrigue him more than a little bit with her bucket list and her eyes that promised something warm and wonderful.

Hell, if he was perfectly honest with himself, he'd admit that something about Lizzy Wiles made him think about sex. Not just regular sex, but the kind of hot, un-bridled, mind-blowing sex he'd never experienced in his life. And he hadn't thought about any kind of sex since long before he'd buried his wife.

And he didn't want to think about it now.

He'd go get Lizzy, let her ride one of his most docile horses, and then he'd take her back to her cabin and be done with it…with her. Then he'd go back to being what he'd been before she'd eaten that piece of pie, a miserable man who was responsible for not one, but two beautiful, vibrant women's deaths.

He frowned. For just today he didn't want to think about that. He didn't want to be that man. Today he simply wanted to be the person helping Lizzy to accomplish something on her bucket list.

He shook his head as he thought about the promise she told him she'd made to her dying mother. It made a strange kind of sense, he supposed, to try to accomplish all the things you wanted to in the area of fun and adventure before you settled down or got too old to enjoy them.

Daniel had never wanted anything more in his old age than this ranch, his family surrounding him and a quiet peace of simple goals achieved warming him deep in his heart.

Now he wouldn't have even that. He'd have no wife, no children to fill the empty spaces around him. He'd live the rest of his life alone and with the regrets of a man who had made too many mistakes.

A half an hour later as he drove toward the Cowboy Café, he thought again about Lizzy's bucket list. Maybe part of the reason he'd responded to her, why he'd decided to spend a little time with her, was because he knew she wasn't any kind of a threat to him on an emotional level.

She was in town for only a little while and had made it very clear that she had things she wanted to accomplish. Once her list was complete, she'd probably drift back to her hometown of Chicago.

It wasn't the same as spending time with any of the single women in Grady Gulch, who might think any interest he showed them was evidence that he was available for a new commitment with one of them.

Never again, he thought as he tightened his grip on the steering wheel. He'd never marry again. He'd never try love again. Emotionally he wanted to stay dead. It was not only what he desired, it was what he deserved.

Still, he couldn't control the slight burst of anticipation that shot through him as he drove around the back of the café and saw Lizzy standing in front of one of the four small cabins.

Clad in a pair of jeans that hugged her long slender legs and wearing a bright yellow T-shirt that made her light brown hair look darker and richer, the sight of her wrestled up a spark of life that had been absent inside him for a very long time.

The minute she saw him, a wide smile curved her mouth, and for a brief moment he wondered what those full lips might feel like against his own.

Don't even think about it, he commanded himself as he pulled his truck to a halt. He didn't even want to go there. She opened the passenger door and jumped into the seat with that bright smile that warmed some of the Arctic air that had been inside him for so long.

"Good morning," she said cheerfully. "I thought maybe you wouldn't show up." She reached for the seat belt.

"Why would you think that?" He waited until she was buckled in and then put the truck into gear.

"I don't know, I just thought you might have changed your mind between Friday night and this morning."

"If I'd have changed my mind, I would have called you and let you know. I wouldn't have just not shown up this morning and left you hanging." He pulled away from the cabins, acutely conscious of the scent of her, the fragrance clean yet with a slightly spicy kick.

"I'm so glad you did show up. I've been looking forward to this all weekend. I can't wait to see your horses." Her exuberant energy shimmered in the cab of the truck. "Have you always lived here in Grady Gulch?"

"All my life," he replied. "I live on the ranch where I grew up."

"And I'll bet you learned to ride a horse by the time you started first grade."

He flashed her a quick smile, the rarely used expression feeling slightly alien on his lips. "Actually, I learned to ride when I was three, but I got my first horse on my second birthday. My dad bought her for me. I named her Cat. Apparently my verbal skills were limited at that time."

She smiled. "And your parents? Are they still here in town?"

"No, they're both gone. My mom passed first. She had a heart attack and died five years ago. My dad had a stroke six months later. I think he just missed her too much to keep living."

He'd much rather talk about her than about his own life. "What about you? You mentioned that your mother had passed away. What about your father?"

"My parents divorced when I was six," she replied.

"So, your father wasn't in your life?"

"Sometimes he was, sometimes he wasn't. He was in and out throughout my childhood. I learned fairly early on not to depend on him, not to expect him to show up when he said he would. In the last seven years, after I turned twenty-one, he's pretty much been out of my life."

"And you're okay with that?" He flashed her a quick glance, noting how the morning sun pulled faint blond shiny highlights from her hair.

"To be honest, I don't spend a lot of time or energy thinking about things and people I can't control, and my father was definitely one of those people. Oh, what a beautiful place," she exclaimed as Daniel turned onto the long driveway that led to his house.

It had been a long time since Daniel had seen his home through a stranger's eyes, but now he found himself filled with an unexpected surge of pride as he gazed at the large two-story house that rose up out of the lush lawn and surrounding green pastures.

The white house with the dark green shutters was old, but Daniel had been vigilant over the years at maintenance and repairs. The paint was fresh and clean, and the house radiated a sturdiness that spoke of endurance.

The outbuildings were also white with green trim.

He realized the whole place breathed with a pastoral peacefulness he used to feel deep in his soul but hadn't felt in a long time.

"It must have been wonderful growing up in a place like this," Lizzy said as he parked the truck in front of the house.

"I had a great childhood here," he said. "Come on and I'll show you around."

As he got out of the truck, he was surprised by the fact that he felt somewhat at ease. She was easy to talk to, open and friendly and, best of all, very temporary, he reminded himself.

She joined him in front of the truck and drew in a big drink of the air. "Smells good enough out here to bottle and wear on your skin."

Although Daniel agreed that the air smelled wonderful, it didn't compete with the slightly exotic scent that emanated from her. "I imagine it's definitely different than the smell of Chicago."

"Since leaving Chicago, I've smelled a lot of cities and small towns, and every place has a distinctive smell." She grinned at him, her eyes sparkling with good humor. "And some are definitely better than others. Grady Gulch will go on my list of good scents."

He motioned toward the barn and corrals in the distance. "You make a lot of lists?" he asked as they began to walk.

She turned to look up at him, as if surprised by the question. "Yes. I never thought about it before, but I guess I do. Oh, I don't write them down, but I do keep mental lists in my head. Smells I like, foods I dislike, places that make me feel warm and places that make me feel cold and so on."

"Will Grady Gulch go on your places that make you cold or places that make you warm list?" he asked, more than a little bit fascinated by the workings of her mind.

"Definitely on the warm list. It's a wonderful small town where people seem to genuinely care about one another. You can feel the friendliness, the caring when you walk down the streets of Grady Gulch."

Not for men like me, he thought. Grady Gulch had definitely been a cold place for him since the night of the tragic accident that had forever changed his life.

"Aren't they beautiful." Lizzy danced two steps ahead of him as they approached the corral, where five horses grazed peacefully in the morning sun. She turned to look at him, her pretty features radiating excitement. "Which one am I going to ride?"

"That all depends on which one chooses you," he replied.

She looked up at him as if curious, and he couldn't help but notice the length of her long eyelashes, the delicate curve of her jawline. "Chooses me?"

He nodded. "My dad always believed that the relationship between a person and a horse was a sacred thing and that it was far more important for a horse to choose a person than a person to choose a horse." He stopped short of the corral fencing and motioned her forward. "Go on, just stand at the fence and we'll see what happens."

Even though she gave him a questioning glance, she not only walked up to the corral but also stood on the bottom rail of the fence, making him realize for the first time that she was probably not much taller than five foot three. Funny, anytime he'd thought of her over the past week, she'd been taller, much bigger in his mind.

"What now?" she asked as the horses pranced on the far side of the corral.

"Patience," he replied, deciding he definitely enjoyed the way her tight jeans cupped her rounded bottom.

"Not particularly my strong suit," she replied with a laugh.

He took a step closer to her. "But it's a must when you're dealing with animals."

He wished he would have had more patience that night. For just a moment Janice's face flashed in his head, a frozen frame of the last time he'd seen her. Her blue eyes had flashed with frustration, her mouth thinned with exquisite anger. If he'd just managed to find a little patience that night then maybe the end result would have been very different.

"Look, they're coming closer."

The vision of Janice in Daniel's head snapped away, and he was grateful for Lizzy's voice brimming with excitement to bring him back from the edge of his dark memories.

Lizzy appeared to vibrate with animation as the mares came closer to their side of the corral. As he watched her, felt the energy wafting from her and noticed the way her hair sparkled in the sunshine, he was determined that for the rest of the day he wouldn't let thoughts of Janice intrude.

For just this single day he'd allow himself the unusual indulgence of feeling something other than his own sorrow and guilt.

Today he was going to allow himself to enjoy a woman named Lizzy and for a little while remember what it was like to truly be alive.

Lizzy had a feeling Daniel was looking at her butt. Even though she was trying to stay focused on the magnificent animals in front of her, she was intensely aware of the magnificent man behind her. And she could swear as she looked at the horses she could feel the heat of his gaze on her behind.

She was just about to turn her head around to see if she was right when one of the horses broke away from the others and approached where she stood on the fence. The chestnut-colored horse held her ears forward, as if curious to hear whatever Lizzy might have to say.

"Hi, baby," Lizzy said softly. The horse had beautiful eyes and moved even closer, flaring her nostrils precariously close to Lizzy's face. Lizzy stood frozen, unsure what to do. The horse neighed softly.

"That's Molly, and it looks like she chose you," Daniel said as he stepped up beside Lizzy.

"What's she doing with her nose? It looks like she's trying to inhale me," Lizzy exclaimed.

Daniel gave a short, deep laugh. "She's taking in your scent. That's how horses identify each other." Molly neighed again as if to punctuate his sentence.

"So, what happens now?" Lizzy asked, ridiculously pleased that she'd been chosen at all. Also the short but sweet sound of Daniel's laughter tickled her.

"And now we're going to take Molly into the barn and you're going to do a little grooming on her. That will help build some trust between the two of you."

Lizzy watched as he opened the corral gate and grabbed a rope that was coiled on the post. It took him only a minute to get the horse out of the corral, and she followed after them as he led both the horse and her into the barn.

The barn was huge and held the wonderful country odors of hay and leather, of horse and grain, but Daniel's woodsy cologne and clean male scent had teased her since the moment she'd climbed into his truck.

He looked hotter than ever today in his jeans and a gunmetal-gray T-shirt that perfectly matched his eyes. He'd seemed tense when she'd first gotten into the truck, but she'd felt him relaxing with each mile they'd driven.

Now he appeared completely at ease, his features relaxed in a way she'd never seen before, and it only made him more attractive. "This is a currycomb," he said as he handed her a soft bristle brush. "You use it in a circular motion on her. Normally I don't groom them until after a ride, but Molly loves to be groomed, and if you do a little now it will assure her that you're a friend."

For the next few minutes she worked on the horse with Daniel instructing her. Although she tried to stay focused on the task at hand, it was impossible with Daniel so close to her. His body radiated an evocative heat, and several times he placed his hand over hers to show her how to move the brush, causing her heart to bump up its rhythm in response.

"Okay, let's saddle her up and we'll take a ride," he

said. She was almost grateful to know that within minutes they'd be on two different horses and separated by enough space that she'd be able to take a full breath. Standing so close to the handsome man made her feel as if she wasn't getting enough oxygen.

It took another twenty minutes for him to saddle Molly and the black horse he was riding for the day, whose name was Dandy. "Are you nervous?" he asked when it was time to get on the horses. They stood just outside the barn with a gentle early June breeze that stirred his thick, slightly curly hair.

"A little," she admitted as she looked up at the back of the horse. "It looks like a long way down from the saddle to the ground."

"Molly is sweet as sugar and you won't have to do much but hang on to the reins or the saddle horn. If you've ever seen a Western movie then I'm sure you know how to get on a horse, but I'll stand right here in case you need some help."

There he was, standing so close to her she could smell the heady scent of him, felt as if she wasn't getting quite enough air to survive. She quickly placed her left foot in the stirrup and with a burst of adrenaline pulled herself up and over, using the saddle horn for leverage.

"You're a natural," Daniel said, obviously pleased by how easily she'd made it into the saddle, which creaked with an oddly comforting noise beneath her weight.

"Thanks," she replied and leaned forward to stroke Molly's neck and then grabbed the reins loosely in her hands. "Now, you be a nice girl and don't make any sudden moves."

Daniel laughed again, that low, deep rumble that Lizzy found amazingly wonderful. "You'll be just fine," he assured her as he easily mounted his horse. "Just relax and go with the movement of the horse."

As Dandy moved toward the open pasture in the distance, Molly followed right behind without Lizzy having to do anything. It took a few minutes for her to get accustomed to the motion of the horse, but she did as Daniel had told her and just relaxed to enjoy the ride.

The horses walked side by side at a leisurely pace, and for several minutes neither Daniel nor Lizzy spoke. Lizzy merely enjoyed the breeze on her face, the novelty of her first horseback ride and the beauty of the land that surrounded them.

Still, there was no way she could keep her gaze from darting to Daniel. He definitely looked as if he belonged on the back of a horse. His posture was relaxed, and yet he seemed completely in control of the entire area around him.

"Do you work all this by yourself?" she finally asked to break the comfortable silence between them.

"Pretty much, although I do hire in or barter for some extra help at different times of the year."

"Must take a lot of work to run a place like this."

He flashed a full smile, and the power of it warmed her from head to toe. "So does waitressing. I guess if you really like what you're doing, it doesn't feel so much like work."

"Point taken," she agreed. "And you love doing this."

He nodded. "It's pretty much all I've ever known, but

yes, I love it. I never really wanted to do or be anything else other than a rancher."

"That's what life is all about, finding your happiness," Lizzy replied. "Did your wife like to ride?"

"No." The smile that had warmed his features only seconds before vanished, and Lizzy mentally cursed herself for bringing up a subject that so obviously filled him with sadness.

"It's a beautiful day," she said after she thought too long of a painful silence had reigned. She hoped to bring that smile back to his lips.

"Probably not as nice as those California days you had selling surfboards."

"Sun and surf are vastly overrated, as far as I'm concerned. California is beautiful, but it's not the place for me. Besides, I got tired of the sand. It gets into everything."

"When you've finished with this bucket list of yours, will you return to Chicago?" He looked at her with curiosity.

"Probably," she replied after a short hesitation. She shrugged. "It's what I know, where I grew up. I guess it makes sense for me to end back up there."

"And will you return to the same kind of work you were doing before?"

Lizzy frowned as she thought of going back to the ad agency. "I don't think so. I'm not sure what I'll eventually decide to do, but it will definitely be something that I love and something that gives me time to enjoy things other than work."

"Ready to go a little faster?" he asked.

She flashed him a challenging grin. "However fast life takes me, I'm always more than ready." She swallowed a squeal as Dandy took off at a gallop and Molly gave chase. Lizzy grabbed onto the saddle horn and held on for dear life.

Once again as her body found and meshed with the rhythm of the horse, a thrilling exuberance filled her. They galloped for several minutes. The wind through her hair, her very first gallop on a horse and the sight of Daniel just ahead of her, everything combined to create one of those moments she knew would go on her list of best experiences ever.

Across a fenced area in a separate field, she saw another cowboy on a horse in the distance. Daniel raised a hand in the air in greeting and the other man waved back.

They slowed to a walk once again when they approached a thick grove of trees. He pulled his horse to a stop and Molly stopped, as well.

"That was absolutely thrilling," she exclaimed.

He laughed. "And that wasn't even a run." He dismounted with graceful ease. "There's a stream here and a pretty place I'd like to show you. We'll let the horses take a little breather, take a little walk and then head back. Can you get down on your own?"

He moved closer to Molly's side, and suddenly Lizzy didn't want to get down on her own. She wanted his big, strong arms around her as she slid from the horse's back. She wanted to get up close and personal with the heady cologne and clean maleness that had dizzied her senses whenever he got near her.

"I'm not sure," she said.

"Same way you got up only backwards. Don't be afraid. I'll catch you if you fall."

As she swung her right leg back to dismount, she was actually grateful for his arms reaching up for her as she nearly fell backward.

She felt herself with her back sliding down his broad chest and his big, warm hands on her arms until her feet hit the ground. His nearness felt so good, and there was nothing more she wanted to do than lean back against him and intensify all the crazy, thrilling sensations that danced through her entire body.

He quickly stepped away from her, and when she turned to look at him his face gave nothing away to indicate that he'd felt anything remotely similar to what she'd just experienced. "Let me show you the stream," he said and began to walk on a well-worn path through the trees.

Lizzy followed close behind him, wondering what in the world was wrong with her. Why was she feeling such a sharp edge of desire for a man who was so obviously off-limits? A man whose heart was still so bound to a woman he'd lost.

It was apparently some wild and crazy hormonal thing, some quirk of chemistry that she just needed to ignore. He led her to a small clearing that was bisected by a clear stream. Wildflowers dotted the area and with the full-leaved trees surrounding them, she felt as if she were in a secret garden.

"Oh, Daniel, this is beautiful," Lizzy said.

"My dad used to call this place his chapel." He

pointed to a large rock that jutted up from the edge of the trickling clear water. "And that was his thinking rock."

"He sounds like a wonderful man." A wistfulness shot through her as she thought of her own father, who had been reliable only in his complete and utter unreliability. "The two of you were close?"

Daniel nodded. "Both my mom and dad were great." He motioned her to the thinking rock, where she sank down as he leaned with his back against one of the nearby tree trunks.

"And you were an only child?" she asked.

Once again he nodded. "And I'm guessing you were an only child, too."

"Yes, it was just me, although for a while I pretended I had a little sister. I drove my mother crazy, kind of like the imaginary friend scenario." She smiled at the memory. "I made Mom set a place for my sister at the table. She had to be buckled into a seat belt in the car. I even tried to make Mom punish baby sister Sarah for things I had done."

"How did that work for you?" he asked with a touch of humor lighting his eyes.

"As you can imagine, it was never Sarah sitting in time-out, it was always me," she said ruefully.

A bird sang from somewhere nearby and the leaves of the trees whispered with the breeze. "This is such a peaceful place. Do you come here a lot?" she asked.

"I used to. Not so much anymore. Spring is a pretty busy time around the ranch, so it's been a while since I've been here."

"And here I am taking you away from all your work," she replied.

He smiled again, that breathtaking grin that she thought she would never get tired of looking at. "Spring is behind us and summer is here. Summer is the time to kind of kick back and just watch things grow."

"That sounds nice." There were things she'd like to ask him, about his past, about the woman he'd lost, but she told herself that not only did he not seem open to discussing anything like that, she shouldn't want to know anything personal about him. Besides, she didn't want to steal that easy smile from his mouth, see the tension creep back into his shoulders by bringing up uncomfortable subjects.

"Who was that you waved to in the other pasture?" she asked, more to keep the conversation rolling than any real curiosity.

"One of the Benson brothers. Their place is next to mine. Do you know them?"

"Sam and Adam come into the café pretty regularly," she replied.

"There's a third brother, Nick. He's the youngest, but he left town a while back and hasn't been back." Daniel shoved his hands into his jean pockets. "I imagine Mary told you about what happened to my wife and Cherry Benson."

Lizzy nodded. "She told me there was a car accident and both women were killed. I'm so sorry for your loss." The words sounded inadequate even to her ears.

"Thanks. What about you? Any marriages in your

past or present?" he asked in an obvious attempt to swerve the conversation away from his tragedy.

"No marriages past or present," she replied. "Not even any close calls."

"Really?

"Oh, there's been a few very brief relationships, but nothing serious."

"Not the marrying kind?" he asked.

"I'm not sure. I guess I haven't met the right man yet, and right now I'm not looking for him."

He pulled his hands from his pockets. "The bucket list."

"Exactly."

They both fell silent, and this time Lizzy didn't feel the need to fill the silence with meaningless chatter. She leaned her head back and closed her eyes and listened to the rush of the wind through the leaves and the murmur of the stream flowing over stones.

"If I were you I'd spend a lot of time in this place," she finally said. She opened her eyes and found him staring at her intently.

The peace and quiet of the little clearing snapped with energy as, for what felt like an infinite period of time, they gazed at each other. Lizzy's heart banged hard and fast as she felt herself leaning forward slightly, as if unconsciously wanting to get closer to him.

"We should probably head back in," he said as he looked away and straightened from the tree trunk where he'd been leaning.

Lizzy rose to her feet, reluctant to leave this place of peace and the man she'd momentarily shared it with, the man who she could swear had just a little bit of hunger in his eyes as their gazes had locked for that instant.

When they stepped out of the woods, she saw that the horses were near where they had left them. "They don't just run away or head back to the barn if you leave them alone?" she asked.

"Some of them will." He watched as she got back into Molly's saddle, then he mounted his ride. "I have one mare who, if I leave her alone for a split second, runs for home no matter where she is in the pasture. Twice I was stuck walking back to the barn from wherever I'd been out in the fields because Nelly-Bell took off without me."

Lizzy laughed as she envisioned him cursing his way back to the barn to scold the wayward Nelly-Bell. "Poor Nelly-Bell," she said. "She's just a homebody kind of girl."

"Guess so," he agreed.

As the outbuildings, the barn and the house came into view, Lizzy was surprised that she didn't want the day to end. It had to be around noon, but he hadn't mentioned anything about lunch. *He didn't invite you for lunch,* a little voice reminded her. All he'd invited her for was a ride on a horse.

And she shouldn't want anything else from him. He was a checkoff on her bucket list, and that's all this would ever be. As they reached the barn, Lizzy realized some of the darkness had crept back into Daniel's eyes and tension was back in his shoulders.

"This was really nice, Daniel. Thanks so much for

taking the time out of your day for me," she said minutes later as they walked toward his truck.

"No problem."

He seemed to have pulled into himself as they'd gotten off the horses. His eyes had shuttered, his expression once again set in stone.

There had been several times during the morning that she'd seen the true Daniel Jefferson shining through. A sparkle in his eyes, a wry lift of his mouth into a smile. She liked that man.

The man leading her back to the truck was the one she'd watched for four weeks come into the café and order two pieces of peach pie, a man more than half broken by grief. He had to be thinking about his wife, about what he'd lost.

"You know, I've always heard that old saying that you should get back up on the horse that threw you," she said when they were in the truck. "I hope after enough times passes you can get back on."

He started the truck and then darted a quick gaze at her. "What are you talking about?"

She pointed to the house. "Your home looks beautiful and is obviously meant for a family. I hope at some point in the future you can put your sadness behind you, find love again and fill that place with children and happiness."

"Never going to happen," he said firmly as she saw his hands tighten on the steering wheel. "I have no desire to ever marry again."

Lizzy wasn't sure why the thought of him forever alone, forever with those haunted gray eyes, filled her with such sadness, but it did. And that, more than anything, made her realize she needed to stay away from Daniel Jefferson for the remainder of her time in Grady Gulch.

Chapter 4

"What are you doing here this morning?" Mary asked Lizzy on Wednesday morning as she walked sleepy-eyed through the back door and into the café kitchen. It was five-thirty in the morning and the sun was just beginning to faintly light the eastern sky.

"Hi, Lizzy." Junior Lempke stepped out of the walk-in refrigerator with a slab of bacon in his hands. He kept his gaze on the bacon as his cheeks warmed with color.

"Hi, Junior." She smiled at the big, sweet-tempered guy who was more child than man and then turned back to answer Mary. "I switched shifts with Brenda for today." Lizzy stifled a yawn with the back of her hand.

"Oh, that's right." Mary pulled a rack of golden-brown biscuits out of the industrial-size oven and set the tray on a cooling rack. "She has a doctor's appointment this morning. Her knee has been giving her fits."

Lizzy nodded and yawned again. "I don't know how she pulls herself out of bed each morning to work this shift. When my alarm clock went off, I was sure it had to be a mistake."

Mary smiled. "Brenda has been working the morning shift for years. She loves getting up before the sun and working breakfast." Mary checked her watch. "And Candy should be here anytime."

"I'll go ahead and get things ready for the early birds," Lizzy said.

"And pour yourself a cup of coffee. You look like you could use a little caffeine bounce," Mary called after her as she left the kitchen and went into the dining area.

"Definitely coffee," Lizzy muttered to herself, and she went to the warmers that were already filled with several pots of the freshly brewed liquid.

She poured herself a cup, took a sip and then got busy checking the area she'd work to make sure everything was ready for the morning crowd. The café would open exactly at six, and there were regular customers who would be standing at the door waiting when Mary unlocked it to officially start the day.

It took Lizzy only minutes to make sure her station was ready for action, and then she did a quick run-through of the tables Candy would work, making sure napkin holders were filled, salt and pepper shaker lids were screwed on tight and tables were neat and clean.

She wasn't surprised that Candy was late. The young girl always complained about being scheduled for the morning shift on Wednesdays. But then, Candy complained about everything, Lizzy thought.

When she was finished with everything, Lizzy paused to take a few more sips of her coffee, trying hard not to think about the man who had been uppermost in her thoughts since their horse-riding time together on Monday.

On their ride back to her cabin, he'd said very little and she'd babbled on like a fool about the nice weather and how much she'd appreciated him letting her ride Molly. The whole time she'd known that he had shut down, turned off and probably wasn't listening to anything she had to say.

When they'd reached her cabin, he'd told her he'd enjoyed their time together. She'd thanked him again and then got out of his truck and watched as he'd pulled away.

Had she mistaken that look of hunger she'd thought she'd seen in his eyes when they'd been in the clearing? Had she only imagined it because she'd felt more than a little bit of hunger for him?

It was definitely time to leave Grady Gulch behind, she told herself as she finished her cup of coffee. It was time to leave because there was a part of her that wanted to stay, a part of her that wanted to see more of Daniel Jefferson, and that wasn't a good thing.

Her intentions were to wait until the weekend and then give Mary her two-week notice. It was time to move on from the little town that she feared had the potential to bewitch her and the man whose personal tragedy and dark eyes would haunt her for a long time to come.

A rap on the door of the café drew her attention from

her inner thoughts. Even though it was still a few minutes before time to open, Mary hurried toward the door where Sheriff Cameron Evans stood peering in.

Mary unlocked the door to allow him inside. "Morning, Cameron," she said, and Lizzy noticed the faint peach color that slid into Mary's cheeks.

"Mary," Cameron replied, his voice low and deep, and Lizzy thought she heard more than a little bit of longing in his voice as he said Mary's name.

Mary relocked the door then turned and walked behind the counter as the sheriff followed and slid onto a stool. Lizzy busied herself wiping down a table she knew was already clean as she watched the morning ritual between the sheriff and her boss.

Mary poured him coffee and the two of them small-talked for a moment, and then Mary disappeared into the kitchen. But, during those few minutes of chitchat, there was no question that there was a simmering tension between the two.

For the past four weeks Lizzy had found it interesting to watch Mary and the handsome Cameron interact. It was obvious the single Cameron was very interested in Mary, and although Mary was friendly with him, there was no question she kept up barriers against him.

The only thing Lizzy knew about her boss was that her husband had died years ago, and like Daniel, Mary had sworn she wasn't open to ever having another romantic relationship.

What was it about people closing themselves off to love? Lizzy only hoped that in both Daniel's and Mary's cases they eventually allowed themselves to love again.

And Mary certainly couldn't do better than the man who kept the law in town, the man who looked at her as if he'd gladly take an order of her to go.

"None of your business, Lizzy," she muttered beneath her breath. Her business was the fact that the café was ready to open in the next couple of minutes and still no sign of Candy.

She moved behind the counter and topped off Cameron's coffee. "How's the crime-fighting business?" she asked.

"Just the way I like it, slow and easy." He smiled, but she noticed his gaze shot through the pass window as if to catch a quick glimpse of Mary. "And how's the waitressing business?" he asked, his focus back on Lizzy.

"Fine, but it won't be long before I'll be heading out of Grady Gulch."

He looked at her in surprise. "I'm sorry to hear that. I thought you were probably going to stick around. I know Mary will be sorry to see you go. She's told me how much she enjoys both you and your work ethic."

"Mary has been wonderful to me," Lizzy said. "And I love Grady Gulch, but this was never meant to be a destination, rather just a pit stop along the way."

Mary reappeared from the kitchen. "Lizzy, I'm about to open the door and it seems that Candy must have overslept…again. Would you mind running to her cabin and getting her up and over here? We're going to need her in another hour or so when the real breakfast rush begins."

"No problem," Lizzy replied.

Mary moved closer to her. "I'd send Junior but he's

already started cooking, and besides, it would take him ten minutes to get up the nerve to knock on her door, and by then he will have forgotten what I sent him there to do."

"I don't mind banging on her door to get her lazy butt out of bed," Lizzy replied.

As she went through the kitchen, her thoughts returned to Daniel. She would probably see him again on Friday night and she wondered what he would order, two pieces of peach pie or an apple and a peach? An apple would be an open invitation for her to join him for a few minutes at the booth.

It was absolutely ridiculous for her to want him to order her a piece of pie, for her to want to believe that he'd had as much trouble getting her out of his mind as she'd had in getting him out of hers.

She left the café and noted that the sun had now made a full appearance in the morning sky and it had already warmed up by several degrees since she'd come into work thirty minutes ago. It was going to be a hot June Oklahoma day.

She didn't even want to think about how crabby Candy would be if Lizzy had to wake her. Candy was cranky on most of the days when she *wasn't* pulled from her beauty sleep.

Knowing that she was working the morning shift, Lizzy had gone to bed early the night before and, much to her chagrin, had dreamed about Daniel. They had been a series of hot, wild dreams of the two of them making love, and when she'd awakened she'd been almost disappointed to find herself alone in the bed.

She reached Candy's cabin and knocked on the door. "Candy, it's me, Lizzy. Hey, girl, you're supposed to be at work right now. The café is opening in about two minutes. Wake up and pull yourself together."

She waited for a response but heard nothing coming from inside the cabin. "Candy." She knocked again, this time harder, and to her surprise the door creaked open a little bit. "Candy?"

Maybe she'd never come home the night before and hadn't realized that when she'd left for the evening her door wasn't closed all the way. But, Candy was always here at night, she thought. Candy had no place else to go. Her boyfriend lived with his parents, and she wasn't from Grady Gulch.

All these thoughts flew through her head as she stood at the door and wondered if she should just walk in or not. Maybe Candy was in the shower and couldn't hear her. She finally decided to walk in.

"Candy?" she called one more time as she entered the room. The smell hit her first, the coppery scent of blood. The unmistakable odor assailed her just a moment before she saw the waitress.

Candy was in the middle of the sofa bed, her eyes staring sightlessly up at the ceiling. She was dressed in jeans and a pink blouse and blood.

There was so much blood. Lizzy's legs threatened to buckle beneath her as she tried to make some kind of sense of the scene before her.

Move, her brain commanded, but she was frozen in place, frozen by horror. This wasn't right. What had happened here? Her brain couldn't take it all in.

With a sobbing gasp, on trembling legs she backed out of the cabin, her heart racing so fast that a sickening nausea rose up inside her. She choked against it.

Dead.

Candy was dead.

Somebody had killed her.

Oh, God, while Lizzy had slept peacefully in her cabin next door last night somebody had come in there and killed Candy. Or this morning while Lizzy had stood in the small shower stall enjoying a bracing shower to wake up, somebody had been inside Candy's cabin cutting her throat.

Run!

Lizzy's mind roared with the command. Move! Finally her brain made contact with her limbs. She hadn't realized she was crying until she whirled around and headed for the back door of the café, suddenly aware that her vision was misted with tears.

She burst through the back door and raced past the kitchen, where Junior was flipping strips of bacon with a fierce look of concentration. He didn't even look up from the grill as she ran past him.

Bursting into the dining area, she collided with one of the stools, which instantly crashed to the floor. "Lizzy!" Mary cried in alarm as Lizzy grabbed hold of Sheriff Evans's arm.

"Candy… She's dead," Lizzy gasped. "She's been murdered."

He jumped off the stool and ran toward the kitchen, with Mary close behind him. Lizzy collapsed onto the stool he'd vacated and hung on to the counter, trying to banish the terrible vision of Candy that lingered in her head.

Several people stood at the front door, expecting their early morning cup of coffee and maybe a plate of biscuits and gravy. They had no idea of the drama that was going on out back. They would know soon enough, she thought as she heard the sound of sirens in the distance. The sheriff had probably called in his entire five-man force.

Who could have done such a terrible thing? Was it possible Candy's boyfriend, Kevin, had killed her? Had they had one of their legendary fights? One that had reeled wildly out of control?

What if it hadn't been Kevin? What if it had been some crazed predator who thought the women in the little cabins would be easy prey? And if that were the case, why Candy's cabin? Why not Lizzy's or Courtney's?

She shivered, colder than she'd ever felt in her entire life as her thoughts careened into dark places. She realized that all she really wanted at that moment was strong, warm arms around her, somebody holding her close and telling her it was all going to be okay.

Unfortunately, the only man's arms she wanted around her were the arms of a man who still had his around the wife he'd lost.

"You hear about the murder over at the café?" Leah Jennings, the clerk in the hardware store, asked as she rang up the new set of bolts Daniel was buying to replace a rusted set in the barn.

"Murder at the café?" Daniel looked at Leah in surprise. "What are you talking about?"

"Seems that one of those gals who lives in those cabins behind the café was killed sometime in the middle of the night." Leah leaned toward him, her eyes wide behind her glasses. "Murdered," she whispered.

Daniel's heart lurched sickeningly, and he backed away from the cash register on legs that had turned to wood. "What? Who?" He felt a roar in the back of his head as a vision of Lizzy standing in front of one of those cabins filled his head.

"I'm not sure which one of the girls. I've been stuck here in the store and haven't had a chance to get over to the café and get the full scoop. Mike Mathews came in a little while ago and said the café had been closed all morning and through noon, but it's open now."

Daniel had stopped listening when she'd been unable to identify which woman had been killed. The roar in his head grew louder as he stumbled toward the front door of the store. "I'll be back later," he said as he flew out of the door and headed for his truck.

Not Lizzy. Please don't let it be Lizzy, he begged as he ran down the sidewalk to where he'd parked his truck earlier to run some errands. As he got into the truck and started the engine, he felt almost light-headed with his fear.

Lizzy was so filled with life, with a bubbling energy that he'd found intoxicating, he couldn't imagine somebody taking away her light.

Maybe Leah was wrong. Why on earth would anyone want to harm any of the women who lived in those little cabins? Maybe some wild rumor had inexplicably flown around the streets, a rumor that had nothing to do with reality. It wouldn't be the first time and it probably wouldn't be the last time wrong information had been spoken as the truth.

It took only minutes for him to drive down Main Street to the east side of town, where the Cowboy Café was located. The time was just a little past two in the afternoon, usually when the lunch rush had ended and the parking lot began to clear.

But the lot was still crowded with cars and trucks, and that alone at this time of the afternoon told him that something was amiss. He found a parking spot and pulled in, his heart pounding so loud in his ears he could hear nothing else.

Not Lizzy. Please not Lizzy. It was a mental mantra that thundered through him as he left the truck and ran for the door of the café.

As he flew through the door his gaze automatically tracked through the crowd, seeking a single glimpse of the woman that would slow his heartbeat to a more normal pace, that would ease the roar in the back of his head.

He saw Mary standing behind the counter, her pretty features strained and her eyes showing the obvious aftermath of tears. Lizzy usually worked the counter. Why was Mary there when Lizzy should be there? Everything else fell away as Daniel tried to control an inner tremble and approached her.

"Mary?" Her name came out of him on a hoarse gasp. "Lizzy?"

Mary pointed to the far side of the café to a small table for two. A sweet rush of relief whooshed out of Daniel as he followed her finger and saw the woman he'd most needed to see sitting alone, her shoulders hunched forward as if she were trying to disappear into herself.

He beelined toward the table, and when he was still several feet away, she turned her head as if she'd sensed his very presence in the room.

Her eyes brimmed with unshed tears and she looked achingly fragile. As he took the last few steps toward her she stood, and when he was within reach, she threw herself in his arms and began to sob.

Daniel stood stiffly for a moment, stunned by her actions, by her very nearness, and then his arms moved up to embrace her. She burrowed against him, her face hidden in the front of his T-shirt as she continued to cry.

As his relief at finding her alive and the shock at having her so intimately close to him slowly ebbed away, he tightened his arms around her and lost himself in the vanilla scent of her hair, the warmth of her body against his and a sharp pleasure he knew he shouldn't be feeling under the circumstances.

He'd forgotten the simple pleasure of a woman's body so close to his, of how female curves felt when fitted so intimately against his own male physique.

As her crying began to ease, he became aware of other things, such as the fact that the café was quieter than usual in spite of the crowd and that people were darting interested glances in their direction. He'd just wanted to make sure she was okay. He hadn't expected to have her in his arms.

She finally raised her face to look up at him, and a hysterical half sob, half laugh escaped her. "Oh, Daniel, you really shouldn't be in here like that. You still have your hat on."

"I don't think Mary will mind this time," he replied, surprised that he felt oddly bereft as she stepped away from him and sank down in the chair where she'd been seated before he'd arrived.

He pulled his hat from his head and walked back to the wall of hooks by the front door, where he hung it among the many others already there.

When he returned to the table, he sat in the chair opposite Lizzy. "Are you okay?" He still didn't know exactly what had happened or who had been murdered. He only knew he was grateful it hadn't been Lizzy.

She nodded. "I found her. She was dead in her bed and there was so much blood…so very much blood." She looked positively haunted, her eyes so dark it was as if the horror of what she'd seen had crept deep inside her.

"Who? Who was killed?" he asked.

"Candy." Lizzy's eyes welled with tears. "Somebody cut her throat, Daniel."

Shock winged through him as he thought of the waitress who had served him so many times. Murdered? He couldn't remember the last time there'd been a murder in Grady Gulch. "Does Cameron know who did it?"

"He's not saying. They've been working out in her cabin all morning and Cameron has been in and out of here questioning people, but that's all I know right now." Her eyes were so dark as she looked at him. "It was awful, Daniel. I don't think I'll ever get that vision of her out of my head."

He wasn't conscious of reaching across the table until one of her small, trembling hands was in his on the tabletop. "I'm so sorry you had to be the one to find her."

She gave a curt nod and squeezed his fingers. "It wasn't exactly one of the things on my bucket list." She released his hand and leaned back in her chair, looking weary and yet frightened.

"Have you eaten anything today?"

She looked at him blankly for a moment. "No. To be honest, I haven't even thought about food."

Daniel looked around, noting that Mary must have called in most of her staff to handle the crowd and cover for the traumatized Lizzy and the missing Candy. He motioned to Dana Maxwell, one of the waitresses buzzing around the tables. She hurried over to him, order pad in hand.

"How ya doing, hon?" She gave Lizzy a sympathetic smile.

"She needs to eat something, Dana," Daniel said.

"Course she does," Dana agreed. "Poor little thing."

"I'm fine," Lizzy replied.

"How about a bowl of soup?" Daniel didn't wait for Lizzy's response. "Yeah, a bowl of that chicken rice soup for her and a burger for me." He was hoping that she'd not only eat some of the soup but might also pick at the French fries that would come with his burger. It was almost three o'clock, which meant she'd already missed two meals.

"Coming right up," Dana replied and left the table.

"How do you know if I even like chicken and rice soup?" Lizzy asked when the waitress had left.

"Everyone likes chicken soup," he replied, glad to see a bit of a spark back in her eyes.

She shrugged as if it didn't matter to her and released a deep sigh. "I just can't believe I was right next door sleeping while somebody was killing her. Maybe if I hadn't been sleeping so soundly I might have heard her cry out and been able to help her."

The very idea of Lizzy running out of the safety of her own cabin and into Candy's to confront a killer chilled him to his very bones. "Thank God that didn't happen, otherwise we might be sitting here talking about two dead waitresses."

Lizzy nodded and looked toward the counter, where Mary stood with an arm around her son, as if attempting to shield him from anything harmful or ugly. Unfortunately, there was no way to keep from the young man that a murder had occurred in his backyard.

"Mary has been really upset about all this. She was going to keep the café closed all day, but people kept showing up at the door and finally Cameron encouraged her to go ahead and open up the doors. I think he wanted to force her to think about work instead of the murder, at least for a little while."

"Maybe *you* need to think about something else for a little while," Daniel said gently.

"It's hard to think about anything else. I hate to say it, but I'm hoping her boyfriend is responsible and that the case is all tied up in a neat and tidy bow by the end of today."

"Who was she dating?" he asked.

"Kevin Naperson."

Daniel frowned. "The Napersons are good people. Tom works as the postmaster and his wife, Nadine, works for the mayor. I hope you're wrong about their son. It would destroy them if he's responsible for this."

"All I know is that Candy used to tell us that Kevin liked to drink a lot and the two of them fought like cats and dogs."

"I'm sure Cameron will figure it all out," Daniel said in an effort to smooth some of the tension that had her nearly vibrating in the chair.

At that moment Dana arrived at their table with his orders. She placed the soup in front of Lizzy and the burger and fries in front of Daniel. "Let me know if you need anything else," Dana said just before she hurried to tend to the needs of other diners.

"Murder is good business," Lizzy said as she looked around the café. "I've never seen this place so busy at this time of the day." He was pleased when she picked up her spoon and dipped it into the soup.

She ate several spoonfuls of soup and then set her spoon down to open a package of crackers. "I don't know what's drawing more attention, me for finding her body or you just sitting across from me right now." Her gaze held his steadily. "What are you doing sitting across from me right now?"

"I heard about the murder while I was in the hardware store. Leah, the store clerk who was working, didn't know who had been killed but knew it was some-body who lived in the cabins." His throat seemed to narrow a bit. "I was afraid it was you. I just wanted to make sure that you were okay." He was surprised by how difficult it was for him to admit that not just to her, but to himself.

Her hand reached across the table and covered the back of his. He was pleased to realize her fingers had warmed up in the past few minutes.

"Thank you," she said simply. She glanced down at their hands for a long moment and then pulled hers away from his and once again leaned back as if in an attempt to get a little distance from him.

"I was going to give Mary my two-week notice this weekend, but I'm wondering if maybe this isn't a sign that it's time to move on from here right away."

"Surely Cameron is going to want you to stick around for a while," Daniel protested.

She looked at him in surprise. "I don't know why. I've told him everything I know about the whole situation. All I did was have the misfortune to be the first person to knock on her cabin door this morning."

"But, now isn't the time to leave." He glanced toward the counter and wondered what in the hell he was doing. He looked back at Lizzy. "Mary needs you right now. She's just lost one waitress, and she's looking pretty fragile."

As she turned to gaze at Mary, once again Daniel wondered why in the hell he was trying to talk any woman, but especially this woman, into staying in Grady Gulch.

Chapter 5

The day was hellish and Lizzy thought it would never end, but end it finally did. When Mary turned the sign in the door from Open to Closed at ten that night, all Lizzy wanted to do was curl up in a fetal ball and sleep for at least the next twenty-four hours.

The only people left in the café were Mary, Cameron, Lizzy and Courtney, who held her sleeping son in her arms. The sheriff looked as if he'd aged ten years throughout the day. They all sat around a table as Cameron sipped the last of the coffee before heading out for the night.

"We processed the scene and got every fingerprint, hair or fiber we could. Hopefully we've got something that will identify the killer," he said.

"Did you talk to Kevin Naperson?" Courtney asked.

Cameron nodded and expelled a weary sigh. "I've

got to tell you, when I spoke to him he seemed shocked and genuinely broken up about her death."

"Yeah, but did he mention where he was between one and three last night?" Lizzy asked. She'd heard the town coroner had pinned Candy's death between those hours of the early morning.

"In bed at his house. According to what Kevin told me, he and Candy went to The Corral last night, but they had a big fight and he dropped Candy off at her cabin around ten. I've got dozens of witnesses that saw them arguing and then leave the bar around that time."

The Corral was a bar on the other end of town. Lizzy had been there a couple of times since arriving in Grady Gulch. It was a huge place with a large dance floor that on the weekends was filled with two-stepping or line-dancing cowboys and cowgirls.

"Anyway," Cameron continued, "according to Kevin, he went back home, where he said he and his father watched a couple of movies and then went to bed around one. Tom, Kevin's father, confirmed the story, and I have no reason to believe Tom would lie to cover for his son, but we're going to look at everything and everyone until we have an answer."

He took another sip of his coffee. "And Candy never talked about another man? Maybe somebody giving her trouble here at the café or around town?"

Almost in unison the others told him no. "And if there was anyone giving her problems, trust me, Candy would have said something about it," Lizzy said. "Candy wasn't one to hold things inside."

"Are we safe staying in the other cabins?" Courtney asked.

"There's no reason to believe you aren't," Cameron replied, his expression dark. "The method of the kill looked…personal. But, I'll have one of my deputies do hourly drive-bys all night long just to make you feel comfortable."

He drained his coffee cup and stood. "I've got to get out of here. I've got reports to write and a crime to solve."

Mary walked him to the door as Lizzy and Courtney remained seated at the table. "I don't want to sleep in my cabin tonight," Courtney said softly. "I'm just so creeped out about all this, and an hourly patrol doesn't make me feel any better."

Lizzy knew exactly how she felt. "Why don't we stay together tonight in my cabin? We can have a slumber party."

"Are you sure you wouldn't mind?" Courtney looked down at the sleeping little boy in her arms. "I can't guarantee that he'll be this quiet all night long."

"I don't mind at all, and if he wakes up and wants to play, then we'll play. Neither of us has to come in tomorrow morning, so it will be fine."

Lizzy realized she didn't want to be alone through the rest of the long night. She'd almost hoped that Daniel would have offered to stay with her, or would have invited her home with him when he'd left after dinnertime. But, a small part of her knew that either scenario would have been foolish for both of them.

He'd been right about one thing. There was no way

she would tell Mary tonight that she was leaving town. As Mary returned to the table, Lizzy noticed how achingly fragile her boss looked, how her hands trembled as she picked up the cup Cameron had recently held.

"What a day," she said, her blue eyes still haunted.

"It's like a horrible nightmare," Courtney said. "Only when we all wake up tomorrow morning, we'll realize it wasn't just a bad dream."

"Hopefully by this time tomorrow night Cameron will have the person responsible in jail and we can all relax," Mary replied. "I can't imagine what Candy's parents are going through."

Her face paled and Lizzy knew she was probably thinking about her own son, Matt, who had gone to bed only minutes before. Mary got up from the table. "Either of you want anything from the kitchen before I call it a night?"

"Not me," Lizzy said. Courtney shook her head. "Courtney and I have decided to have a slumber party tonight and stay in my cabin together." Lizzy got up from the table and touched Courtney's slender shoulder. "Come on, girl, let's get out of here so Mary can go to bed."

It was nearly an hour later that Garrett slept peacefully in the playpen Courtney had set up next to the sofa sleeper in Lizzy's cabin and the two women sat on the pullout bed in their pajamas, talking in low tones so as not to disturb the little boy.

"I still can't believe she's gone," Courtney said. "And no matter what Sheriff Evans says, I think Kevin did it. It's the only thing that makes any kind of sense."

Lizzy nodded and desperately tried to keep her last vision of Candy out of her head. "Hopefully it will be like Mary said, by tomorrow night we'll know who killed her and whoever it is will be behind bars."

"I'm just glad we're staying together tonight," Courtney said with a glance at her son. "I was just too freaked out tonight to want to stay by myself."

Lizzy pulled her knees up to her chest and wrapped her arms around them. "Trust me, I wasn't looking forward to being here all alone tonight."

"If you'd played your cards right you might have had a handsome man here in this bed next to you instead of me," Courtney said teasingly. "Everyone who was in the café all day couldn't miss how Daniel and you were together."

Lizzy's cheeks burned as she remembered those moments of being held in his arms, of his hard masculine body so close to hers. She'd wanted to stand in his strong, warm embrace forever.

"I'll admit that I have a crazy attraction to him," Lizzy replied.

"He didn't exactly look completely immune to you, either," Courtney replied. She tucked a strand of her long dark brown hair behind one ear. "I think everyone was shocked to see him with you today. He's been totally shut off from everything and everyone for a long time."

"It's just a friendship kind of thing," Lizzy replied, although the jump in her heart whenever she thought of him or said his name aloud told her otherwise. "Besides, it doesn't matter that he was there for me today. I'm leaving town soon, and he's still hung up on his wife. That's a festering wound, and who knows if it will ever heal."

"Even so, it's nice to see him coming alive again. He's never been the same since the car accident." Once again Courtney's gaze went to Garrett. "Nothing has been the same since then."

"I know Garrett's dad isn't in your life, but is he in the area? A homegrown boy?" Lizzy desperately wanted to talk about something other than murder, and she didn't want to think about Daniel because thoughts of him pulled forth a deep yearning inside her that was almost scary.

"He's a homegrown guy," Courtney replied after a long moment of hesitation. "But, he doesn't know about Garrett. He left town before he even knew I was pregnant."

"So, he doesn't know he's a daddy? Don't you know where he is? Can't you get in contact with him to let him know?" Lizzy knew that Courtney was estranged from her parents. The young woman had nobody to help her, either financially or emotionally.

Courtney's pretty features hardened. "Even if I could call him to tell him right now, I don't think I would." She sighed and her eyes filled with pain. "Daniel's life wasn't the only one that changed with that damned car accident. Garrett's father is Nick Benson, but you have to promise you won't tell anyone that. Nobody knows this."

Lizzy looked at her in surprise. "Nobody knew you and Nick had something going on?"

Courtney shook her head. "It's a long story and I

don't want to go into it now, but no, nobody knew Nick and I were dating, and then he left town on the day of Cherry's funeral and I've never heard from him since."

There was no disguising the bitterness that laced Courtney's voice as she said his name. "And he broke your heart," Lizzy said softly.

Courtney nodded and then lifted her chin. "But, I'm so over it. I'm so over him. I don't know about you, but I'm exhausted."

An hour later Lizzy was still awake in the darkened room. She could hear the sound of Courtney's breathing, soft and rhythmic in sleep, but no matter how hard Lizzy tried to fall asleep, it just wasn't happening.

Her mind was still too filled with the day's events, with thoughts of Candy and murder, and Mary trying to hold everyone together. She stared up at the dark ceiling as she thought of what Courtney had told her about Garrett's father.

It was amazing how a single incident in a life could have such a rippling effect for so many people. The accident that had claimed Daniel's wife and her best friend had not only broken Daniel but had also apparently affected Courtney, as well. And it would continue on with Garrett, who might never know his father unless something happened to change that.

Every action had a reaction and people touched other people's lives in unexpected and unforeseen ways. When she left Grady Gulch she would take a piece of the handsome, sad cowboy named Daniel with her, and she wondered if her brief sojourn into his life would leave them better or worse than they'd been before she'd arrived in town.

It was almost ten when Lizzy awoke the next morning, surprised to find herself alone in the cabin. A note next to her on the bed let her know that Courtney had gotten up early and she and her son had gone to their own cabin and she'd be back later to get the playpen when she was sure Lizzy was awake.

Lizzy got out of the sofa bed and headed for the bathroom, eager to get showered and dressed and head into the café. She wanted to know the latest on Candy's murder. Hopefully the news was that the murderer was behind bars.

Half an hour later as she made the walk from the cabin to the back door of the café, she wondered if she'd see Daniel today. There was really no reason to believe that she would. The only reason he'd come in the day before was because he hadn't known who the victim had been. There was no reason to believe she'd see him before tomorrow night when he made his usual Friday night trip.

As she walked into the kitchen she saw Rusty Albright manning the grill. He cast her a quick, sympathetic glance. "Morning, Lizzy."

"Good morning, Rusty. What's the news?" Lizzy asked.

"There isn't much," he replied. He flipped a couple of pancakes over and then turned to look at her. "Sheriff hasn't been in this morning, although I heard from the grapevine that the only suspect on his list at the moment is Candy's boyfriend." His blue eyes grew dark.

"I just wish I would have heard something, could have somehow helped Candy. I was right there in that cabin and slept through that poor girl's death." He shook his head and turned back to face the grill.

It was the longest conversation Lizzy had ever had with the man, but she knew exactly how he felt. She felt the same way. "I'll talk to you later, Rusty," she said just before she left the kitchen and stepped into the dining area.

She slid onto a stool at the counter and smiled at her boss, who set a cup in front of Lizzy and then filled it with coffee. "Thanks," Lizzy said. "Any news?"

Mary shook her head. "Nothing worth reporting." Mary looked around the buzzing café. "We've been busier than usual this morning and there's been a lot of rumors flying around, but that's all they are."

"You need me to suit up now instead of waiting until two?" Lizzy asked. "I don't have any plans for the day."

Mary gave her a grateful smile. "If you don't mind, that would be great, and then maybe I can let you off early this evening."

As Lizzy went back to her cabin to change into her Cowboy Café T-shirt to work, she told herself that the only reason she was sticking around for a while longer in Grady Gulch was because Mary needed her. It had nothing to do with Daniel Jefferson, nothing to do with him at all.

For the next several hours Lizzy had no time to think of anything or anyone but serving the customers who came in for the lunch rush.

It was just after four in the afternoon when the Benson brothers came in and slid into a booth in the section where Lizzy was working.

"Hi, Sam…Adam." She greeted the two handsome men with a smile and tried not to think about the fact that the brothers had a little nephew they didn't even know existed.

"Hey, Lizzy," Sam replied with a smile. "I hope you're doing better today than yesterday."

"A little," she replied. "Although I'd be doing better if I knew somebody was in jail for Candy's murder."

"We'd all feel better if that was the case," Adam said.

"What can I get for the two of you?" Lizzy asked.

She'd just finished taking their orders when she looked up and saw that Daniel had entered the café. Instantly Lizzy's heart stepped up its rhythm.

She placed the order at the pass window and then walked back to where Daniel had slid into one of the booths in her section. "You're making this place quite a habit," she said in greeting.

He smiled at her. "I could have worse habits."

The warmth that his smile sent through her gave her both a thrill and a warning. She couldn't get mired in the warmth of that smile, in the very charm of him and the growing feelings she had for him. "What can I get for you?"

"Pot roast the special tonight?" he asked. "And do you have time to take a break and eat some with me?"

Currently there was a small lull in the café traffic, and Lizzy had a feeling if she was going to get a break in before the dinner rush it had better be soon. "I'll check with Mary. Anything to drink?"

"Iced tea."

Fifteen minutes later, with the rest of her customers momentarily taken care of and with two pot roast specials in her hands, she went back to his booth. She served him and then slid into the booth, across from him.

"How did you sleep?" he asked. "You look tired," he added before giving her an opportunity to reply. His gaze was intent on her face, creating a hot pool of desire in her stomach as she threatened to fall into the beautiful gray depths of his eyes.

Her mind exploded with the memory of being in his arms the day before, of feeling his heart beating strong and steady against her own, the very scent of him both an intoxicant and a soothing balm.

Before he'd shown up the day before and she'd thrown herself in his arms, she'd felt hauntingly alone, with only the visions of Candy to keep her company. His presence had banished the horrid visions and his embrace had warmed all the cold areas inside her.

"Lizzy?"

Heat filled her cheeks as she snapped back to the here and now. "Oh, I slept fine," she said after remembering what he'd just asked her. "Courtney and her baby stayed in my cabin with me. If I look tired it's because I've been here working since a little before eleven today."

"Is Courtney staying with you again tonight?"

Lizzy shook her head and picked up her fork. "No. Last night we were both a little freaked out by everything, but we're both feeling better…stronger today." She cut into the tender roast. "Talk to me about normal things, Daniel. Tell me about things at the ranch." She'd heard about nothing but murder all day and was hungry for something else, something of Daniel's world.

"Molly told me to tell you hello," he said as he picked up his fork.

Lizzy gave him a rueful smile. "It seems like it's been months since I took that ride with you, and it's only been three days." She shook her head and popped a piece of carrot into her mouth. "Tell me more."

"The sunrise was nice this morning. I drank my coffee on the back deck and watched it rise. It was peaceful." He looked at her as if surprised. "It was the first time I've felt peaceful in a long time." He leaned back in the booth and averted his gaze out the window. "Anyway, it wasn't long and the chickens were squawking and morning had arrived and there were chores to be done."

Lizzy gazed at him, noting the strength that radiated in his features, a solid capability that rode his broad shoulders. "I had a terrible time getting to sleep last night," she said. His gaze swung back to meet hers. "And the one thing that finally made me fall asleep was thinking about that beautiful clearing you took me to. Thank you for that."

"You're welcome." He cleared his throat, and for the next few minutes they focused on their meals. As they ate they compared notes about the rumors each of them had heard throughout the day.

"I've heard everything from a crazed psychotic drifter to her parents hired a hit man who was responsible for Candy's death because she moved here," Lizzy said.

Daniel raised a dark eyebrow. "I hadn't heard the parent theory."

"I'm hoping that particular rumor has a swift death," Lizzy replied. "Can you imagine being a grieving parent and hearing nonsense like that?" She shook her head and looked up as a tall, beautiful blonde woman and a broad-shouldered, dark-eyed cowboy came toward their booth. Immediately Daniel's shoulder stiffened and he sat up straighter in the seat.

"Daniel." The blonde nearly sneered his name. "Unusual to see you here on a Thursday evening," she said.

"The food is good here no matter what day of the week you eat it," he replied.

The woman's gaze flicked over Lizzy as if she were a piece of lint that marred the beauty of an expensive black dress. She returned her gaze to Daniel. "I'd say it's nice to see you, but you know better than that." She turned to her tall male companion. "Come on, Denver. Let's get out of here." The couple headed toward the front door.

"Wow, who was that?" Lizzy asked after the two had disappeared from sight.

"The woman is Maddy Billings and her friend is Denver Walton."

"She doesn't appear to be much of a fan of yours." Lizzy saw the tension slowly releasing from his shoulders.

"She isn't. Maddy was close friends with Janice and Cherry," he replied.

Lizzy frowned. "So, why is she so mad at you?"

He released a small sigh. "It's a long story."

"You're the second person to tell me that in the last twenty-four hours," Lizzy said, thinking that Courtney had told her the same thing when talking about Nick Benson. "Doesn't anyone have a short story to explain things?" she added in frustration.

"The short story is that Maddy never wanted Janice to marry me and she blames me for Janice's and Cherry's deaths." He shoved his plate aside, finished with the food and apparently finished with that particular conversation. "Since you came in early today, is Mary letting you off early?"

As the bell over the door tinkled to announce new arrivals, Lizzy looked around the place and then shook her head. "It's doubtful. Everyone in town seems to be making their way here to find out if anyone else has heard anything about the murder. I think the dinner rush is going to be massive, and we'll probably stay busy until closing time."

"Maybe what you need in the morning is to get out of here and take another ride with me at my place. I could pick you up around nine and have you back here for your two o'clock shift."

She shouldn't accept the offer. He was getting too far under her skin, too deep into her heart, and it would only make it more difficult when she left here, when she left him.

"That sounds wonderful," she said, despite all her misgivings to the contrary. She told herself that she didn't have to worry about getting in too deep with

Daniel. After all, it took two to tango, and Daniel was still emotionally dancing with his dead wife.

He wasn't offering her anything more than a horseback ride and friendship. The fact that she felt all kinds of crazy emotions and desires for him was her problem, and surely she could control herself where he was concerned until the time she left town.

"Good, then I'll pick you up around nine," he replied. "Maybe we'll have a picnic lunch in the clearing."

"That would be terrific."

The meal was finished and Lizzy knew it was time for her to get back to work, but she was reluctant to leave him. *Get a grip, Lizzy,* she thought to herself. It wasn't as if she wasn't going to see him again. She'd see him first thing in the morning.

With a burst of adrenaline, she slid out of the booth and reminded herself she had a bucket list to complete and this was just a stop along the way. "Then I'll see you in the morning," she said briskly as she gathered their empty plates in her hands.

By the time she'd taken the dishes into the kitchen and returned, Daniel was gone, and for the next two hours Lizzy worked a dinner rush busier than ever before.

Lizzy saw several unfamiliar faces, men and women who probably rarely dined out or had never been in the café before. She figured they were probably there to get the latest facts about Candy's murder. But, there were no facts to disseminate. Neither Cameron nor any of his deputies had made any appearances in the café all day long.

It was just after nine when Cameron finally came through the door, the wear and tear of the day evident in the tired lines that creased his face.

He flashed Lizzy a weary smile as he made his way to the counter, where Mary poured him a cup of coffee. Lizzy moved to join them, obviously eager to hear what the official news was from the lawman.

"After everyone pounding the sidewalks all day long, interviewing everyone in this one-horse town, I still just have one potential suspect...Kevin," Cameron said with obvious frustration.

"Then why don't you just arrest Kevin?" Lizzy asked.

Cameron turned to look at her with tired eyes. "Because right now I don't have any concrete evidence to do so. It's all circumstantial at the moment. He has an alibi, and I don't even have the murder weapon."

"So, what happens now?" Mary asked.

"We keep digging. Sooner or later if Kevin is guilty, he'll tell somebody what he did, or we'll find the weapon or we'll be able to destroy his alibi. It's just a matter of time before we get a real break in the case."

"You look exhausted," Mary said, and Lizzy saw the softness of her boss's eyes as she gazed at him. Lizzy moved away from the counter, giving the two people time to speak alone.

By nine-thirty the café had begun to clear out. Exhaustion weighed heavily on Lizzy's shoulders, and for the first time since she'd been working at the café her feet hurt. For nearly eleven hours she'd been dashing to serve and clean up after the diners. It had definitely been a long day.

Mary had offered to let her off an hour before, but Lizzy had insisted Mary send Courtney home early, knowing that Courtney still had to drive to her baby-sitter's house to pick up her son before settling down for the night.

The fear and the horror connected to Candy's death had become more distant today. It was tragic. It was horrifying, but Lizzy truly believed the culprit was Kevin and it was just a matter of time before Cameron had the young man behind bars.

It was just after ten when Lizzy finally stepped out of the back door of the café to head to her little cabin. The light she'd left on earlier served as a beacon to welcome her back to the comfort of her bed, and at the moment that's all she was looking forward to—sleep.

There were also lights in Courtney's and Rusty's cabins. Only Candy's was dark, and Lizzy felt that sad, piercing darkness deep inside her soul.

Even the night around her seemed darker than usual as she began the walk to her cabin. Candy had been so young. Death should never have been anywhere near her.

Lizzy was halfway to her own cabin when she thought she heard something behind her, a faint pad of a footstep, a sense of movement that was out of place.

Before she could turn around to check it out, an arm wrapped tight around her neck and she felt herself being pulled back against a hard, firm body.

She had no chance to scream, no opportunity at all to even squeak in protest. The arm smashed against her windpipe, making it impossible for her to release a scream or draw any air in.

Panicked, she kicked backward to try to hit her attacker, tried to somehow twist away from the killing grip he had around her neck, a grip that was stealing the very last of her oxygen from her brain, causing a weakness to possess her.

Who was doing this? her mind screamed. Why were they hurting her? As she thought of Candy's murder, the terror inside her spiked to hysterical levels.

"Leave town, bitch," he whispered against her ear.

She wanted to scream to him that leaving Grady Gulch was exactly what she intended to do. She needed to break his grip around her neck and explain that she had a bucket list to complete.

But, there was nothing she could do…. Her body had taken on a bonelessness as dark shadows began to edge in around her thoughts. Oh, God, he was choking her to death, she thought wildly. She was going to die here. She'd be dead, just like Candy.

The sound of a sharp female scream split the night, and for a brief moment Lizzy thought that she was making the noise, that she had finally found a breath of air to sound an alarm.

But, as a scream came again, she realized it was Courtney. The pressure around Lizzy's neck eased. "This is your warning. Get out of town, Lizzy," the attacker snarled in her ear, and then suddenly he released his hold on her and shoved her forward.

Lizzy crashed to the ground, her knees and arms taking the brunt of the fall. She was vaguely aware of footsteps running away from her, feet running toward her, but she remained unable to move except for drawing in deep gulps of sweet, desperately needed air.

"He attacked her." Courtney's voice was hysterical. "I saw it. He had her around the neck."

"Lizzy, you all right?" It was Cameron's deep voice that spoke. She managed to move her head in an affirmative way without opening her eyes. "Which way did he go, Courtney?"

"He ran that way," Courtney replied.

There were more running footsteps, and then Mary crouched down next to Lizzy and placed a hand in the small of her back. Although Lizzy still had her eyes closed, she knew it was Mary by the soft scent of her familiar lilac-scented perfume.

"Lizzy, are you hurt? Can you get up?" Mary asked softly.

Lizzy opened her eyes and slowly moved to a sitting position, a spasm of coughs overwhelming her for a moment. When the coughing finally stopped, a trembling began in the center of her stomach and slowly worked out, down her arms to her fingers, down her legs to her toes.

In the faint moonlight that splashed down and with her eyes adjusting to the near-darkness, she could see Mary's worried face in front of her, and standing just behind her Courtney looked on, her eyes wide in fear.

"I thought I was going to die," Lizzy finally managed to gasp. She looked past Mary to Courtney. "Thank God you saw me. Thank God you screamed."

"I knew you'd be getting off work, so I was going to

run down to your cabin and grab the playpen," Court-ney said. "I stepped outside and saw you…saw him. Oh, Lizzy, thank goodness I stepped out when I did."

"Did you see who it was?" Mary asked Courtney as she helped Lizzy off the ground.

Courtney shook her head. "It was too dark. I couldn't see his face. I just saw somebody big and with his arm around her neck, and when I screamed he ran off." Courtney's voice still rang with fear. "I've got to go get back to Garrett. I left him in his crib in my room."

As Courtney ran back toward her cabin, Mary led Lizzy toward the café's back door. Lizzy felt as if with each step she took she was just beginning to awaken from a particularly horrible dream.

When they reached the back door, she turned to Mary and stared at her in shock as the full impact of what had just happened slivered through her. Somebody had nearly killed her, and that somebody wanted her out of Grady Gulch.

Chapter 6

Daniel was in the process of heading upstairs to get ready for bed when his cell phone rang. Picking it up, he was surprised to see from the caller ID that it was Mary Mathis.

He answered the phone, his heart racing as his thoughts instantly went to Lizzy. "Mary, what's going on?"

"Everyone is fine," Mary began, these initial words instantly sending Daniel's worry through the ceiling. He clutched the phone tighter against his ear. "Somebody attacked Lizzy as she was leaving work and walking to her cabin. She's shaken up, and I just thought maybe seeing your friendly face might calm her down."

"I'm on my way." He didn't wait to hear another word. All he knew was the driving need to get to Lizzy as soon as possible. Mary thought Lizzy needed him, and that was all that was important.

Within ten minutes he was in his truck and headed to the café, his heart banging painfully hard against his ribs. Attacked. Exactly what did that mean? He should have asked Mary more questions.

Attacked could denote a number of things. Had somebody hit her over the head? Beaten her up? Tried to rape her? As each possibility crawled through his mind, his heart beat faster, more frantically as he pushed on the gas pedal to get to her as quickly as possible.

Whatever had happened to Lizzy, it wasn't so bad that Mary had called him from the hospital, and that was the only comfort Daniel had as he raced toward the café.

When he veered into the parking lot, it was empty except for Mary's car, Sheriff Evans's car and another patrol car. The sight of the official vehicles once again stoked a new raging fear inside him.

As he entered the café, he saw Mary, Cameron and Lizzy seated at a table. Obvious surprise widened Lizzy's eyes at the sight of him.

"I called him," Mary said to her. "I thought maybe you needed him here."

Lizzy's cheeks flushed a faint pink color. "You didn't have to bother him. I'm fine."

"Well, I'm here now," Daniel said as he sat next to her with a nod to Cameron. Besides, as far as he was concerned, Lizzy didn't appear to be fine at all. Her face was chalky pale except for her throat, which appeared angry and red. Daniel wanted to somehow comfort her, but at the moment he was more interested in Cameron getting the answers he needed to apprehend the culprit.

"You didn't sense anyone in the area when you stepped out of the café back door to head to the cabins?" Cameron asked.

"No, nobody," Lizzy replied, one of her hands rising to her throat. "I just took a couple of steps and then I thought I heard something, but before I could turn around he wrapped his arm around my neck, pulled me tight against him and started choking me."

For Daniel that answered his first question of what, exactly, had happened. He tamped down a surge of impatience and reminded himself that if he just listened he'd probably get the full story.

"And you didn't see his face at all?" Cameron asked.

Lizzy shook her head and dropped her hand back to the table. "No. He attacked from behind. I didn't see anything but dark shadows as he squeezed tighter and tighter."

Daniel's stomach knotted as he thought of her helpless and being choked by somebody. Was this attack tied to Candy's murder? Was there some killer out there preying on vulnerable women?

"Did you get any sense of the size of the man? A smell coming from him or any idea of what he was wearing?" Cameron continued.

Lizzy frowned. "No, nothing like that. It all happened so fast. He was definitely tall and strong." Her frown deepened. "But, I'm not sure he meant to kill me. I think maybe he was going to just hold on to me until I passed out."

"Why would you think he wasn't trying to kill you?" Daniel could no longer hold on to his silence. The idea of somebody squeezing the life out of Lizzy not only terrified him, but filled him with an unexpected simmering rage.

"Before he let me go he said that it was a warning, that I should leave town."

Cameron's frown was as deep as Daniel's. "He told you to leave town?" Cameron said.

"He said 'Leave town, bitch. This is a warning, Lizzy, get out of town,' or something like that," she replied.

"'Lizzy'? He called you Lizzy?" Mary looked at her in surprise.

"So he knew you by name," Cameron added.

Daniel could tell by the widening of Lizzy's eyes that she hadn't really processed that information yet. "Yes," she said, her voice fainter than it had been. "He definitely knew me by name. But, if he'd wanted to kill me, I got the feeling he was strong enough to snap my neck like a twig. I really believe it was a warning for me to leave town."

"But, why?" Mary asked in obvious confusion. "Why would anyone want you to leave Grady Gulch? Everyone loves you, Lizzy."

"Apparently somebody isn't a big fan of mine," Lizzy replied darkly.

"Anyone giving you problems? Maybe a customer you fought with?" Cameron asked, and it wasn't lost on Daniel that he'd asked the same kind of questions about Candy after her murder.

"No, nobody," Lizzy replied. "Everyone has been extremely nice to me since I've been in town. There's only one person the whole time I've been here who looked at me like I was a piece of dog poo on her shoes, and I know she wasn't the one who strangled me."

"Who is that?" Mary asked.

Lizzy directed her gaze to Daniel, who answered the question. "Maddy Billings was in earlier." He didn't need to say any more. He knew that both Cameron and Mary knew the history between him and Madison Billings. "Denver Walton was with her," he added.

"If Maddy was going to have her boyfriend strangle anyone, it would be you, Daniel," Cameron said dryly. "Still, I'll check him out."

"Maybe Deputy Collins will find something. Maybe the attacker dropped something as he ran away or left some footprints or something," Lizzy said, a slight edge of desperation in her voice.

Cameron looked at his wristwatch. "He and Deputy Temple should be checking in anytime now."

"You know, I was already planning to leave here in the next couple of weeks. Maybe it's time to move up my timeline," Lizzy said.

Daniel wanted to protest. He definitely hadn't been ready for her to come into his life, but he also knew he wasn't ready to let her go…at least not yet. But, he kept silent.

After all, what right did he have to ask her to stay there and face any more potential danger? He had nothing to offer her and knew that even if he did, she had her promise to her mother to fulfill.

"I know it's a lot to ask, but I'd rather you stick around

here for a few more days," Cameron said. "You're at the center of this particular investigation. You heard his voice, and even though you don't remember anything else specific about him right now, it's possible that once some of the shock wears off you'll remember some little detail that might be important."

Daniel could feel the fear wafting from Lizzy, knew that her natural instinct would be to flee from here, where she had no ties and absolutely no reason to remain.

Still, he knew she would agree to stay because Cameron had asked her to, and Daniel knew he'd never sleep peacefully again with the thought of Lizzy alone in that little cabin behind the café.

"You can stay out at my place," he heard himself saying. "I've got plenty of guest rooms and you'll be safe there." It was impossible to read Lizzy's eyes as she turned to look at him.

"That's a great idea," Mary said before Lizzy could protest. "And I'll get busy hiring a couple of new waitresses to fill the vacancies."

"I'm not a vacancy yet," Lizzy said. "Even if I stay out at Daniel's, I don't intend to quit working here." She raised her chin slightly. "He can chase me away from my cabin, but I'll be damned if he'll make me quit my job before I'm ready to."

"That's up to you," Cameron said, "although I definitely think it's a good idea if you move out of the cabin until we have this all settled."

"What about Courtney?" Lizzy asked. "Rusty can

probably take care of himself, but I don't want her and little Garrett to stay out there all alone."

It touched Daniel that, despite the fact that she was the one who had been attacked, her thoughts were for her friend and her little son.

"I'll get Courtney and Garrett settled in at the motel for the rest of tonight and then we'll figure something out for them more permanently tomorrow," Daniel said.

At that moment Deputies Temple and Collins walked in, both of them wearing expressions of defeat. Daniel felt not only his own disappointment but also everyone else's at the table.

"Nothing," Deputy Collins said with a frown. "We couldn't find anything in the area. We searched in the direction Courtney said he ran and found nothing there, either. He must have run hard and fast, but he didn't drop or leave anything behind that we could find."

Cameron drew a weary hand through his dark brown hair. "Ben, why don't you head out back and see to it that Courtney Chambers gets moved from her cabin to the motel for the night."

"Will do," Ben Temple said and immediately turned and went out the door.

"And Jim, see if you can find anyone who might have seen a car parked around this area, or somebody running down the streets," Cameron continued.

"Do you think this has something to do with Candy's death?" Lizzy's voice sounded smaller than usual as she looked at the sheriff.

He hesitated a long moment. "I don't know. To be honest, it's just too early to tell. If it was the same person who attacked Candy, then I don't know why he didn't wait until you were alone in the cabin to attack you. He took a chance doing it out in the open, where somebody might see. And then there's the matter of the weapon. He used a knife on Candy, but you haven't mentioned him having any weapon."

Lizzy shook her head. "All he had was his arm wrapped tight around my neck."

Cameron rose wearily to his feet. "Right now my gut instinct tells me these are two isolated incidences, but I'm not ruling out any connection between Candy's killer and what happened tonight." He turned and looked at Mary, and his gaze softened. "You make sure you lock up tight here, and we'll continue patrols."

"Our living quarters are secure," she replied.

He nodded. "Make sure they stay that way. Doors locked whether you're in there or not." He turned his attention to Daniel. "Take this woman to your place, where I know she'll be safe for the rest of the night."

"I'll keep her safe." Daniel felt his determination rumble in his chest. Nobody would hurt Lizzy as long as she was with him. He'd make sure of it. He turned to look at her. "Shall we go pack your things?"

She nodded and together they got up from the table. "Call me if you think of anything else," Cameron said as they headed for the back door.

"Trust me, you'll be the very first person I call," Lizzy promised.

It wasn't until they stepped out into the dark of night that Lizzy edged closer to him, as if fear alone controlled her movements.

He hated that. In his brief relationship with Lizzy she'd appeared fearless, and it broke his heart to know that some of that charming courage had been stolen away from her by an unknown attacker.

"Wait here," she said just outside the cabin door. "It will just take me a few minutes to gather up my things."

Daniel stood at the door and listened to the sound of her packing. He stared toward the back door of the café. If he had his way he wouldn't have wanted her to continue working, but it wasn't his call. It had to be hers, and apparently she didn't intend to let anyone chase her away from the café.

What was going on in Grady Gulch? Who was behind these attacks? Like Sheriff Evans, Daniel wasn't convinced that Candy's murder and the attack on Lizzy were related, but the idea that they might be was horrifying.

Lizzy's attacker had warned her to get out of town. Why? Why would her leaving town be important enough to somebody for him to attack her? What would happen if she didn't heed the warning and remained here?

She would be the first woman in his house since Janice had died, and the idea of having Lizzy beneath his roof, albeit in one of his guest rooms, both excited and terrified him.

He'd offered to take on the responsibility of her for safety reasons and certainly had no intention of offering her anything more than room and board, his protection and friendship.

But, he had nothing more to offer her. No matter how much he wanted to taste her lips, no matter how much he wanted her in his bed, he wasn't about to do anything that might make her believe there was a future there with him, not that she'd given any indication that she wanted one.

He just wanted to keep her safe, and he hoped he was doing the right thing by bringing her home with him. The last thing he wanted was to be responsible in any way for another woman's death.

Half an hour later, Lizzy followed behind Daniel's truck in her own car. She had no idea if she was doing the right thing or not by going home with Daniel. His offer had shocked her, and the fact that she'd accepted his offer had equally stunned her. But, there was no question that she was afraid, and the only people she truly trusted in this town were her waitress buddies, Mary and Daniel.

She kept telling herself she needed distance from Daniel, that he was the first person in her travels who held a threat to her plans, to her promise to her mother. He had the potential to be the right man, but it was definitely the wrong time in her life to entertain any kind of romantic thoughts.

Don't be silly, she told herself. He was still tightly bound in love to the wife he'd lost. He'd given her no indication that he was ready to move on. Rather, to the contrary, he'd made it clear that he had no desire to move on with anyone.

He'd offered her a safe haven, and right now that's all she wanted. If she'd had to stay in that cabin, she would have never slept again. She wasn't worried about

Rusty, who was a tough older man, but she was grateful that Sheriff Evans was making other arrangements for Courtney and Garrett.

Get out of town, bitch. The words thundered in her brain, and she clutched the steering wheel with tightened fingers. Who would want her out of town, and why? She wasn't a threat to anyone. She didn't know anything that might harm anyone. She had no secret knowledge that could destroy a marriage or wreck a business. Even though she had discovered Candy's body, she certainly had no information that could point a finger to her killer.

It didn't make sense, and when something didn't make sense it worried her. It also didn't make sense that on some level she was eager to see Daniel's home, to see the things he surrounded himself with every day, things that might tell her more about the man.

And even though she'd be leaving there in a couple of days or so, she wanted to know more about Daniel the man. There was no question that in the week she'd been spending time with him, some of the dark shadows in his eyes had abated.

Mary had warned Lizzy not to break his heart, but what Lizzy feared would happen was that if she wasn't cautious, she'd be the one leaving there with a broken heart.

By the time they pulled up in front of Daniel's house, not only was Lizzy exhausted by the adrenaline that had finally dissipated from her since the attack, but she was also tired of overthinking everything.

She got out of her car at the same time Daniel got

out of his truck. He walked with her to the trunk of her car, where she'd stashed three hastily packed suitcases.

She grabbed the smaller pink toiletry bag while he lifted up the two larger suitcases. They didn't speak as they left her car and walked to his front porch.

He set the suitcases down, unlocked his door and then ushered her inside. She wasn't sure what she'd expected of Daniel's living room, but the homey atmosphere created by overstuffed furniture and dark wood end tables atop a huge braided rug that complemented the gleaming hardwood floors wasn't it.

There was a bookcase against one wall holding a variety of books about ranching and several small bronze sculptures of cowboys. The couch was situated in front of a beautiful stone fireplace, and it was easy to imagine stealing some of the throw pillows from the sofa to lie on the floor in front of a roaring fire. A flat-screen television hung above the fireplace mantel, and Lizzy knew that Daniel probably spent most of his spare time sprawled on the sofa watching TV.

What surprised her more than anything was the absence of photos. She'd expected to walk into a shrine of sorts to Janice, but there was nary a photo of the woman in the room.

"Daniel, this is lovely," she said as she set down her cosmetic suitcase.

He dropped the two suitcases he'd carried in to the floor. "Come on, I'll show you the kitchen."

She followed him in and nearly caught her breath at the size of the room. It was built to be a family kitchen, a place to gather to eat and do homework and connect with each other.

It was painted a cheerful yellow, with yellow-and-white gingham curtains hanging over the windows that allowed the sun to play on a small breakfast nook.

"Cook much in here?" she asked, noticing that both the stovetop and oven had the cleanliness of little use.

He pointed to the microwave and the toaster next to it. "If it can't be toasted, zapped or grilled, then it's not being eaten in this house."

"This is a kitchen meant to be used for family gatherings and big meals," Lizzy said. She turned to look at Daniel, unsurprised to find his eyes dark and enigmatic.

"I'll take you upstairs and we'll get you settled for the night," he said, an obvious dismissal of her observation.

As they walked back through the living room, she grabbed her small suitcase and he once again lifted the two larger ones. He led her up a flight of stairs to the second floor. "Two guest rooms on the right, one on the left along with the bathroom," he said when they reached the landing. "The master suite is at the end of the hall."

He showed her each of the three guest bedrooms, and she took the one on the left next to the hall bathroom. All of them were lovely rooms, but this one made her feel instantly at home with its petal-pink spread and gauzy white curtains at the windows. The furniture was blond, fashioned years ago with the stability of solid craftsmanship.

"This will be fine," she said as she set down the cosmetic bag. He dropped the suitcases just inside the bedroom door.

"You'll find fresh towels and anything else you might need in the linen closet in the bathroom."

She nodded. It was close to midnight and she was sure he was eager to get to bed. A wealth of gratitude swelled up inside her. This man owed her nothing. She was nothing more than a piece of flotsam drifting through his life, and yet he'd stepped up for her, a virtual stranger, who was in need.

She took a step closer to where he stood in the threshold. "Daniel, I can't thank you enough for letting me stay here temporarily." Unconsciously, a hand rose to her neck as she remembered those horrifying moments of not being able to breathe.

His eyes darkened and he took a step toward her. "When I think of somebody hurting you, it makes me sick to my stomach." He balled his hands into fists at his sides. "Honestly, it makes me angry as hell."

Lizzy moved even closer to him and smiled up at him. "I don't believe in anger."

He frowned. "What do you mean, you don't believe in anger?"

She shrugged. "It's just been my experience that anger is an emotion that masks the real emotion beneath it. A wife says she's angry with her husband, but the truth of the matter is she's feeling either frustrated or betrayed. A mother is angry with a child, but it's usually disappointment she's really feeling. Life would be much easier if anger was taken out of the mix altogether and people could be in touch with their true emotions."

He frowned, as if trying to take in what she was saying. "The workings of your mind absolutely fascinate me," he finally said. "So, what is it that I'm feeling right now if not anger?"

She stepped forward again, moving close enough to him that she could feel his body heat radiating outward. "You're afraid for me, and maybe part of what you feel is puzzlement about who would try to hurt me or warn me to get out of town."

"It's a nice theory, Lizzy, but I've got to be honest with you. When I think of somebody wrapping their arm around your neck and squeezing the air out of you, when I allow myself to feel what you must have felt at that moment, I'm just plain pissed."

She smiled at him and at the same time felt the wetness of tears beginning to fill her eyes as she thought of those moments when she'd been certain she was going to die.

This time it was he who reached for her. He pulled her against him and wrapped his arms tight around her back. She melted against his strong chest. Even though she told herself she wanted nothing from him except a little bit of comfort, at that moment, with his heartbeat racing against her own, she knew she wanted more.

He held her as if he never wanted to let her go, and she reveled in his embrace. For the first time since she'd stepped out of the café that night to head to her cabin, she felt safe and protected.

She wanted to stay there forever, to allow time and the very movement of Earth to occur without intruding in their space. She wanted nothing of the outside world to ruin this moment of simply existing in his arms.

All too quickly his arms dropped to his side and he

leaned back from her. He raised a hand and caressed with gentle fingers across her throat. "I wish I just understood why this happened."

"That makes two of us," she replied. She felt half-breathless standing so close to him, with his gaze smoky and intent on her.

"Lizzy, I'm only going to do this once, and that's only because I've been thinking about it since the first time you faced me across the booth," he said.

She knew at that moment he intended to kiss her. His gaze lingered on her mouth, a hot promise in his eyes as he leaned in for conquest.

She hadn't expected this. She wasn't prepared for the kiss, wasn't prepared for him to be in her life here and now, but that didn't stop her from yearning for the feel of his lips against hers.

When his mouth touched hers, his lips were sizzling hot, as she'd known they'd be, but she hadn't expected the hunger that instantly overwhelmed her as she opened her mouth to eagerly accept his kiss.

She had no idea if it was his hunger or her own that roared out of control. She only knew that his tongue whirled with hers in a wild dance of desire and she was lost in the smoking sensuality of him.

She'd expected a kiss to be a simple thing, but there was nothing remotely simple about the way Daniel Jefferson kissed. He nibbled, he tasted and he acted as if it might be the very last time in his life that he had the opportunity to kiss a woman.

He raised his hands to her cheeks, framing her face as if it were an exquisite piece of art. His hands were slightly rough, the hands of a working man, and she loved the way they felt against her skin.

By the time the kiss ended, Lizzy felt like a hot pool of want. Her knees threatened to buckle beneath her with the force of her desire for him.

She thought she saw the same emotion in him, the intense longing for more, but it was there only a second and then hidden as his eyes darkened and he stepped several inches back from her.

"I had to do that once, but it would be foolish for us to allow it to happen again or to take it any further," he said, his voice sounding deeper than usual. "Neither one of us are in a place in our lives where kissing each other makes any kind of sense." He took another step back from her. "So, I'll just say good night."

As she watched him head down the hallway to his bedroom, she knew he was right, but just once in her life she would have liked to be foolish and end up with him in his bed.

Chapter 7

Daniel rode on the back of Dandy the next morning, his thoughts rumbling a hundred miles an hour in his head and in as many directions.

Who wanted Lizzy out of town, and why? Had she flirted with somebody and then spurned him as a potential lover? Had she dated somebody else before spending time with Daniel, and now that person was in some sort of rage?

When he got back to the house he intended to ask her some hard questions in hopes that they would get some answers that made sense of the whole thing.

A smile of amusement lifted his lips as he thought of her theory about anger. Still, as amusing as he'd found the conversation this morning, he was wondering if perhaps there was a lot of truth to what she'd said.

Anger was an easy emotion to grasp on to, one that

masked deeper, more profound emotions inside. Had he been angry with Janice on that fatal night? He'd certainly thought so at the time and in the weeks and months since the accident.

But, now in retrospect, it hadn't been anger that had driven that final argument. On his part, he'd been frustrated and felt guilty with her demands, and he knew she had been impatient and disappointed that he was going to break a promise to her. So many emotions had existed between them, and yet they both had grabbed on to anger to use as a sword against each other.

He shook his head, wanting to, needing to dispel the fight that night that had ultimately led to Janice's death. Besides, it was hard to think about Janice when Lizzy so filled his mind.

That kiss.

That damnable kiss.

It had kept him tossing and turning through the night, wanting more, needing more from Lizzy. She'd become a burning in his soul. Each and every time he was with her he wanted to wrap her in his arms and carry her to bed. She fascinated him with her lists and outlook on life, with her observations of people and emotions.

But, the last thing he wanted to do was bind himself in any way to a woman who would ultimately leave him. He had no desire to experience any kind of heartbreak again.

Lizzy would stay at his place for a couple of days. Sheriff Evans would find out who was responsible for the attack on her, and then Lizzy would be gone and he'd be left the way she'd found him—alone and miserable.

He checked the fencing and then turned Dandy around to head back to the house. It wasn't true. She wouldn't leave him the way she'd found him. With her effervescence and obvious zest for life, she'd breathed a new appreciation of life back into him.

He was ready to move on from the tragedy that he had allowed to define him as a man. It wouldn't be with Lizzy, but at least after she left he'd be open again to socializing with the townspeople, with holding his head up high.

Maybe that had been fate's reason for bringing her to Grady Gulch and to him, to remind him of the joy that surrounded him if he just put aside his guilt and misery long enough to enjoy it.

It was just after eight when he walked into the house and was struck by the scent of warm maple syrup and coffee. He stood in the threshold of the kitchen and watched Lizzy, who had her back to him. She'd apparently found a waffle iron in the cabinets that he rarely explored, and she was humming under her breath as she poured batter into the contraption.

He stood breathlessly still, just enjoying the sight of her. She was clad in a pair of pink pajamas with a robe thrown over the top. Her hair was still slightly mussed, as if she'd hurriedly climbed out of bed, washed her face and then had come downstairs to find breakfast.

He thought he'd never seen a woman who looked so sexy, and he could easily imagine that wonderful scent of warm, half-asleep woman mingling with the residual fragrance of her exotic perfume.

He cleared his throat, uncomfortable with the direction of his thoughts. She whirled around to look at him, and a beautiful smile danced across her features. "Ah, perfect timing. Waffles are going to be ready in about three minutes."

"You don't have to cook for me," he said as he walked over to the countertop that held the coffeemaker.

"And what makes you think I'm cooking for you?" she asked with a teasing smile. "I woke up with a ravenous appetite for waffles. I just figured if I was making them for myself, I'd be nice and make a couple for you, too." She flashed him a quick grin. "Besides, cooking for you is the least I can do since you're giving me safe haven."

He carried a cup of coffee to the table and sat, his gaze lingering on her as she turned back around to attend to the waffles.

He wanted her. Even the knowledge that she'd be leaving town very soon couldn't stanch the need that burned in his stomach. It was as if she hadn't just awakened him to the world around him, but had fired up his hormones to combustible levels.

"Here we are," she said as she placed a platter of waffles in the center of the table. "Now just a little butter and some hot syrup, and we're in business." She poured the heated syrup into a small stoneware pitcher and added it and a tub of butter to the table.

She sat across from him with a cup of coffee in hand. "Dig in," she said. "They aren't good if they get cold."

"Did you sleep well?" he asked as he speared one of the waffles with his fork.

"Like a baby," she replied as she slathered her waffle

with butter. "I was afraid I'd have nightmares, but if I dreamed at all I don't remember. What about you? How did you sleep?" She drowned the waffle in the syrup.

There was no way he'd admit to her that he'd slept poorly, haunted by his own desire, tortured by visions of her in his bed. "I slept okay."

For the next few minutes they focused on the meal, although the sight of Lizzy's lips shiny with syrup was a particular form of torture for him. As her tongue slid across her lower lip to catch an errant dollop of the sweet liquid, Daniel felt his grip on control coming close to snapping.

He ducked his head and focused solely on the meal. The easiest thing for him to do was to pretend she wasn't there. He ate three waffles but still felt a restless hunger inside him that he knew food would never satisfy.

When they'd finished eating he helped with the cleanup, stacking the dishes in the dishwasher after she'd rinsed them. As they worked she chattered about the people who were regulars in the café, about how much she'd enjoyed her time in Grady Gulch and that she thought her next stop would be some mountaintop where she would sit and stargaze.

Each and every word of her conversation was a reminder to him that this was a temporary stop for her, that he would always be nothing more than a temporary man. And wasn't that exactly what he wanted? No ties, no commitments, nobody for him to disappoint.

"I need to get upstairs and take a shower," she said when the dishes were all put away.

"Yeah, I need to do the same," he replied.

"We could always shower together and save water."

She had to be joking, he thought. But as he turned and looked at her, there was no teasing light in her eyes. Rather, he saw a mirrored image of his desire there. It stole his breath away and made his lungs ache in his chest.

She took a step closer to him, her whiskey eyes inviting him to imbibe, to become intoxicated with her. "I didn't tell you about one of the things on my bucket list."

"And what's that?" he asked, aware that his voice sounded half-strangled with his need of her.

"To make love to a man I'll never forget. I believe that you're that man, Daniel. I want to make love to you, and when I leave here I'll have the warmth of that memory of us together to carry with me for the rest of my life."

A memory. That's what he'd be to her and that's definitely what she would be to him and that's all they'd be to each other. Was that so bad? Was it so bad to have a memory of passion to carry with him through the rest of his lonely life?

Her hand slid into his, and at that moment he knew he was lost and he didn't want to be found. They left the kitchen and Daniel felt as if he'd stepped into a dream, a wonderful dream from which he didn't want to awaken.

With each step they took up the stairs he expected her to pull her hand from his and tell him it had all been a silly joke. But, instead as they walked closer to his master bedroom, her hand squeezed more tightly with his.

Daniel had always felt as if the master bathroom was huge, but it shrank to intimate proportions with her so close to him. She took the lead, opening the glass shower door and turning on the faucets. Within moments steam began to rise out of the shower enclosure and fill the room.

She then went to the linen closet and pulled out two large, fluffy towels. She set them on the counter and then turned to gaze at him, her expression suddenly one of hesitation. "If I'm being presumptuous here, then please stop me before I make a total fool of myself."

In reply to her he pulled his T-shirt off and dropped it on the floor behind him. Her eyes widened and then narrowed as her gaze slid across his bare chest. "Covering that chest should be a sin," she said huskily.

Her comment only stoked the flames of desire higher inside him. He watched as she took off the robe and hung it on the hook on the back of the bathroom door. As she began to unfasten the pearllike buttons that ran down the top of her thin, cotton pajamas, the blood in Daniel's veins threatened to boil over.

She shrugged out of the top, leaving her barebreasted, and suddenly Daniel couldn't get into the shower with her fast enough.

He wanted to take a bar of soap and slowly run it across her breasts, down her back, across her slender shoulders. He wanted to wrap her in soapsuds and then slide his body against hers.

He nearly stumbled to the floor in his eagerness to get out of his jeans, quickly followed by his socks and boxers. By that time she was gloriously naked, and together they stepped into the shower.

The first thing he did was pull her into his arms, and the feel of her naked body against his own was magic.

It was as if nothing had come before her and nothing would ever come after her. There was just this moment in time and she belonged completely to him.

As the warm water cascaded over their bodies, their lips met in a kiss that made him feel as if he'd never truly been kissed before. He tasted eagerness and heat and the faint sweetness from the maple syrup of the waffles she'd eaten earlier.

He was already fully aroused, and he hadn't even picked up a bar of soap yet. He realized he'd wanted this since the moment she'd slid across from him in the booth and eaten the pie he'd ordered for Janice. He'd known at that moment that somehow Lizzy was going to change his life.

It wasn't long before the bar of soap glided across her bare skin. As he caressed it across her slender shoulders and down her breasts, he couldn't think anymore. He could only experience the wonder of Lizzy.

When they had soaped and stroked and kissed every inch of each other, they finally rinsed off and Lizzy stepped out of the glass enclosure. She wrapped herself in one of the large towels and then handed him one as well. But, he didn't take it from her. Instead he scooped her up in his arms and carried her out of the bathroom and to his king-size bed.

He placed her gently in the center of the navy sheets that held his scent, as if she were the most precious bundle he'd ever carried.

She thrilled, knowing that the best was yet to come. And she was ready for him…soft and yielding and hungry with need. The shower had been an intense form of foreplay, but now she wanted him to possess her completely.

He joined her on the bed and peeled the towel back as if opening a gift to expose her to his hungry gaze. She shivered with emotion as his mouth captured hers again, his kiss holding what words could never say.

As he kissed her, one of his hands explored first one of her breasts and then the other, his work-roughened palms erotic and causing her nipples to rise up to meet him.

There was no question in her mind that this was the lover she would never forget. *Daniel.* His name sang through her head as his hands began to explore her naked body.

When his mouth captured the tip of one of her breasts, she moaned with the sensation. He teased with his tongue, nibbled with his lips until she was half-mad with her desire.

Each touch was fire, and she welcomed the heat that burned away any thoughts of attacks or murders or bucket lists. There was no place in her mind for any thoughts other than of him.

She not only accepted his touch, but was an active participant, thrilling at the feel of his chest beneath her fingers, the sensual pleasure of his bare legs tangled with hers.

It didn't take long before she wanted him not just touching her, not just kissing her, but inside her. She'd been ready for him since they'd gotten out of the shower, and she didn't want to wait another minute.

"Daniel, I want you now," she whispered softly. "I want you making love to me. I want you inside me."

She didn't have to ask twice. His smoky eyes devoured her as he moved on top of her. She parted her legs to allow him between them.

"This is crazy," he murmured.

She smiled up at him and grabbed his buttocks. "Yeah, crazy good."

His neck muscles were taut as he hovered over her, and there was no humor in the depths of his eyes as he slowly eased into her. A small gasp of pleasure escaped her lips, and he caught it with his, kissing her as he slid deeper into her.

When they were fully interlocked, neither of them moved as his mouth trailed down the side of her throat, and she simply took in the sweet sensations shivering through her.

She realized he would be the lover she never forgot because at some point in the past week he'd stolen a little piece of her heart, and when she left there she would feel the absence of that small piece for a long time to come.

Then he moved his hips against hers and all thought fled from her mind. As he thrust into her, she was nothing but tingling sensations and breathless gasps.

He was utterly in control, moving against her in a way to give her the most pleasure possible. He didn't just stroke into her, but moved in circular motions that all too quickly had her spiraling up and up until there was no place else to go but climax and crash down with his name a cry of pleasure on her lips.

It was as if her orgasm snapped something inside

him. He began to move faster against her, pistoning his hips in a frenzy of driving need.

She loved it, the wildness in him, the focused desire to finish what they had begun. And when he reached his own climax, he released a low, deep moan that resonated in her very soul.

For long minutes they remained locked together. She could feel the pounding of his heart against her own. It was one of the sweetest sounds she'd heard in a very long time.

He brushed a strand of hair away from her face. "I didn't even think about protection."

"It's okay. I'm on the pill." She raised her head to gaze at him. "Although I haven't been with anyone for years."

"And I haven't been with anyone since my wife," he replied.

Just that quickly, it felt as if there were three people in the bed: he, she and the wife he'd never forget. Crowded. The bed suddenly felt crowded. She had no idea if he felt it, too. She gave him a kiss on the cheek and then rolled away from him and out of the bed.

She had to get a little breathing room. It had all been too intense, far too wonderful, and she needed some time to gain some perspective.

"I've got to get moving," she said as she grabbed her pajamas and robe and left his bathroom.

"Yeah, me, too. I'll see you downstairs."

She left his room and went to the bathroom in the hallway. She took a quick second shower, hoping to wash away the scent of him, the very feel of his touch against her skin.

She'd only borrowed him for a minute, that's what she had to remember. Hopefully she'd be gone from there in the next couple of days and he would be a check-off on her bucket list. He would definitely be a memory to carry with her, a memory that would last a very long time.

By the time she had dressed and come down the stairs, Daniel was heading out to work in the barn. When he was gone, Lizzy puttered in the kitchen, where she made a tuna salad for their lunch and kept her head as emptied as possible of thoughts.

Lunch talk consisted of ranch things. He told her about future plans to rebuild the barn, to add a stable. His eyes sparkled as he spoke, and Lizzy almost wished she'd be there to see all his plans come to fruition.

But, she couldn't think that way. She'd made her promise to her mother, and she was determined to carry it through. She had places to go and things to see, adventures to complete before she finally thought about settling down into one place.

By one o'clock she was dressed in her Cowboy Café T-shirt and preparing to leave for work.

"I'll drive you to work," Daniel said as he came into the kitchen.

"That's not necessary," she protested. "I can drive myself there and home." What she needed more than anything was some distance from him. He was already under her skin. She didn't want him too deeply in her head, in her heart.

He frowned. "I don't like the idea of you leaving work at midnight and being on the road all alone to come back here."

"Daniel, I'm a big girl. I've been taking care of myself for a long time. It's just a fifteen-minute drive. I'm sure I'll be fine."

"Yeah, and it was just a two-minute walk from the back door of the café to your cabin, and that didn't work out very well for you."

"I'll be fine," she said curtly. Making love to him had been beyond wonderful, but it had also complicated things between them. She saw a new softness in his eyes that threatened to pull her in, and that hadn't been part of the deal.

She picked up her car keys. "You'll probably be in bed when I get home. Would you mind giving me a house key so I can just let myself in when I get home?"

She could tell she'd irritated him by insisting that she drive herself, but he pulled a ring of keys from his pocket and took one off to hand to her.

She put it on her own key ring. "Guess I'll head out. I'll see you in the morning."

She walked out into the hot afternoon air and drew in a deep breath. She had to get Daniel out of her head, get the familiar scent of him out of her nose. Making love with him had made him dangerous to her, because she wanted to do it again…and again.

It was time for her to leave. She hoped Sheriff Evans came in this afternoon and she could get the okay to leave town. She never liked staying anyplace where she might get involved with somebody, anyplace that might seduce her into making it a permanent home.

She feared that Grady Gulch and Daniel were dancing a slow seduction around her, and that frightened her as much as Candy's murderer and her unknown assailant.

Chapter 8

Daniel told himself at dinnertime that the only reason he wanted to head into the Cowboy Café was for dinner and to find out the latest news about Candy's murder and whoever had attacked Lizzy.

But, the truth of the matter was the house had grown quiet…dead without her energy, without her life force in it. If he were perfectly honest with himself, he'd admit that even though it had been only four hours since she'd left, he missed her.

He was doomed, he thought as he got into his truck to make the drive into town. He had that helpless feeling of not her, not now. He was falling for Lizzy, and he knew in his heart she was the wrong woman at the wrong time.

But, it felt so right when he was with her. She made him laugh and she made him think. When she looked at him, he wanted to be the man he saw reflected in her eyes. And it had definitely felt better than right when he'd had her in his bed, when he'd made love with her.

She'd made him look outward again, when he'd been trapped looking inward and mired in his own guilt and feeling of responsibility for Janice's and Cherry's deaths. He still felt that when he had a moment of silence in his mind, but Lizzy was beginning to fill up those silences, and when she looked at him he felt as if he was a better man.

But she didn't know the truth of the night of Janice's death. She didn't know the agonizing details of the fight that had driven Janice out that night to meet her death.

He shoved away these thoughts, not wanting to dwell on anything he couldn't change. Instead he thought of seeing Lizzy again.

It was crazy, how quickly she'd gotten to him, had opened up his heart in a way that made him both wary and exhilarated. He'd like to believe that any woman who had entered his life at this time would have had the same magic as Lizzy, but his heart told him otherwise.

In the past eight months or so there had been several attractive single women who had made it clear they'd be interested in pursuing something with him. But none of them had been able to pierce through the shell of isolation he'd built around himself until Lizzy.

He couldn't help the smile that curved his lips as he found a parking place in the Cowboy Café lot. The smile wavered slightly as he saw Denver Walton's pickup. If Denver was inside the restaurant then Maddy was probably with him, and there was nobody on earth who hated Daniel more than Maddy Billings.

She would always believe he was responsible for Janice's and Cherry's deaths. The two had been on their way to pick her up, and it was only by the grace of God that the wreck had occurred before Maddy got into that car.

As he walked in the door he noticed two things: Maddy and Denver were at a table on the far end of the room, and Lizzy was working the counter.

She flashed him a surprised smile that warmed his heart more than it should. He hung his hat on a hook and then walked to an empty stool at the counter.

"Hey, cowboy, what's your pleasure?" she asked.

He gave her a lazy grin. "I had my pleasure earlier this morning, so I guess I'll just take whatever is on special for now."

Her cheeks pinkened as she charmed him with a blush. "The special is spaghetti and meatballs, and you're a wicked man to talk about your conquests."

He raised an eyebrow. "As I recall, you had a conquest at the same time, and spaghetti and meatballs will be fine."

She wrote his order on her pad. "I'll rustle that right up for you." She turned to the pass window and then turned back around to face him.

"So, what's the news?" he asked.

She frowned. "Nobody seems to know anything new. If Cameron has any leads, he's keeping things close to his chest. I've heard that he's not only questioned Rusty a couple of times, but also Junior."

"Junior?" Daniel looked at her in surprise. "I don't want to sound offensive, but I wouldn't think Junior was mentally capable to pull off a murder without leaving any evidence behind."

Lizzy nodded with a frown. "That's true, but I know Candy didn't hide the fact that she thought Junior was creepy and stupid. More than once she said ugly things to his face."

"Did you tell that to Cameron?" He could smell her familiar scent despite the savory odors of the café. Immediately he thought of nuzzling her neck, of getting up close and personal with the fragrance that drove him half-wild.

"I told him, but like you he pretty much dismissed the idea that Junior is responsible." She leaned closer to him. "You are thinking naughty thoughts. I can see it in your eyes."

He leaned back and laughed and then quickly sobered. "You have no idea how nice it is for me to have naughty thoughts. It's been a very long time since I've indulged myself in any kind of pleasant thinking."

Her gaze softened and she lightly touched the back of his hand. "I'm so sorry that life hasn't been kind to you."

At that moment all Daniel could think about was how unkind he'd been to Janice just before she'd stormed out of the house. Thankfully at that moment one of the customers at the other end of the counter called for her attention.

He was falling for Lizzy, and even though he knew it would lead to nothing but more heartache, he seemed helpless to stop the tumble of emotions she stirred in him.

He thought of what she'd told him about Cameron taking a second look at both Junior and Rusty. Although Rusty had been working for Mary for about three years, Daniel knew very little about the man other than he lived in one of the cabins out back and wasn't prone to friendly small talk.

It was difficult for him to consider anyone in his town capable of doing what had been done to Candy. It was just as difficult to try to comprehend why anyone would half strangle Lizzy and warn her to get out of town. Why? It just didn't make any sense. She wasn't a threat to anyone. She hadn't been able to give the sheriff any information about anything concerning Candy's murder.

By the time she returned to deliver his meal, he couldn't sustain any negative thoughts with her bright smile shining on him. She set his plate before him and then leaned toward him across the counter.

"I think we should start our day tomorrow with a sunrise horse ride," she said. "I'm missing Molly."

"She's missing you, too. She told me so this afternoon after you left for work, and I think a sunrise ride sounds great. If you take her a couple of slices of apple she'll be yours forever."

She gestured toward his plate. "You'd better eat before it gets cold."

"Who's working the grill tonight?" he asked.

"Rusty. Why?"

"I just want you to be careful walking to your car. Until we know who is responsible for the crimes here, I worry about you taking more than two steps alone in the dark."

"I'll be careful," she replied, obviously touched by his concern. "Cameron usually shows up here around closing time. I'll ask him to watch me walk to my car." Then another customer needed something, and once again she moved away from him.

He was halfway through his meal when Sam and Adam Benson came through the door. Adam took the empty stool next to Daniel and Sam sat on the other side of his brother.

"How's it going?" Adam asked.

"Not bad. How about at your place? Things going well?"

"Cattle are getting fat and the corn is almost knee-high." Adam smiled at him. "What more could a rancher want?"

Sam leancd forward to look at Daniel. "Heard any news about the mini-crime wave that's struck the town?"

"Nothing worth repeating," Daniel replied as he cut through one of the large meatballs on his plate. "What about you two? Heard anything?"

"We've heard that Kevin is still the number one suspect and Cameron is trying to find a way to break his alibi. If he can find one person who saw Kevin out the night of the murder after ten o'clock, then the kid is busted."

"But that doesn't explain who attacked Lizzy. Kevin would have no beef with her." Daniel's gaze shot down to where Lizzy was pouring a cup of coffee for Robert McKay, an old-timer who had lost his wife six months ago.

"I think Cameron is looking at them as two unrelated incidences," Adam replied.

"Personally, I can't figure out why anyone would want to hurt Lizzy, but I also don't believe her attack had anything to do with Candy's murder," Sam said.

Although the conversation had been easy, Daniel felt the sorrow that still simmered in the air among the three of them, all who had suffered the tragedy of that car accident almost two years before.

At that moment the object of their conversation returned to take Adam's and Sam's orders. Lizzy was good at her job, friendly but not flirtatious, and she made each and every diner she served feel as if they were her number one priority.

Why hadn't she married? She was open and loving, fun and beautiful. Why hadn't some lucky man snapped her up long before her mother had died and she'd made her bucket list?

It was a question that he suddenly felt he needed answered. She was from Chicago, for God's sake, a city with plenty of single men, and yet she'd told him she'd never been seriously involved with anyone.

She was getting more and more tangled in his heart, and he was beginning to wonder if there was any way he could talk her out of leaving town, talk her into forgetting the rest of her bucket list.

For the first time in a very long time, Daniel was looking for a future, and when he looked ahead he couldn't imagine his days without Lizzy in them.

This thought didn't bring him joy but rather settled a shroud of faint depression across his shoulders. He had a feeling there was no happy ending for him and Lizzy, and if he were perfectly honest with himself he knew he didn't deserve one.

It was just before closing time that Sheriff Evans came into the café. Daniel had left hours before and the café was almost empty of people. Lizzy was seated at the empty counter having a glass of iced tea before leaving for the night.

She got up and greeted Cameron with a tired smile. "How's it going?" she asked as she poured him a cup of coffee.

"To be honest, I've never felt so frustrated with everything. We just can't seem to catch a break on anything." His frown of discouragement instantly arranged into a tired smile as Mary joined them. "I just wanted to stop by and see that you were doing okay," he said to the pretty blonde.

Lizzy believed Cameron showed up each night for a cup of coffee, but more important so that Mary was the last person he saw before going home alone.

It was obvious to Lizzy that the man was heartsick, but it was equally obvious that Mary didn't feel the same way. Whenever she looked at Cameron there was a guarded distance in her eyes, a slightly wary gaze.

For the next few minutes they all talked about the crimes and the discouraging lack of leads Cameron and his deputies suffered.

"My gut still tells me Kevin is good for Candy's murder, but I've got no evidence I can use to make an arrest. Anything I have on him is circumstantial, and he's got an alibi that I have yet to break." He looked at Lizzy once again. "As far as the attack on you, I don't even know where to begin to find answers. Since we can't come up with a motive, it's hard to know where to look for the perpetrator."

"You'll figure it out," Mary said with encouragement.

He nodded and cupped his hands around his mug, his gaze going back to Lizzy. "What I just can't understand is how the attack on you relates to Candy's death."

Lizzy raised her hand to her throat, for the space of several breaths captured in that moment of terror. That arm, wrapped so tight around her neck, slowly cutting off her precious air supply, had been the most frightening experience of her entire life.

She drew a deep breath, shoving past the memory, and dropped her hand back to the counter. "Maybe there's no link to Candy's death. Maybe it was just somebody who didn't like the way I served them that night, somebody who just doesn't like me at all."

"That's impossible," Mary said without hesitation. "You're everyone's favorite waitress."

Lizzy gave her a grateful smile, but she was aware of Cameron studying her intently. "Are you sure there's nobody from your past? No ex-boyfriend who might have tracked you here?"

"No, there are no boyfriends in my past." Both Mary and Cameron looked at her in surprise. She shrugged with a wry grin. "What can I say? I was totally focused on my work for years, and since my mother's death I've been traveling around too much to pick up a boyfriend along the way."

"Until now," Mary said softly.

Lizzy felt the blush that swooped into her cheeks. "Daniel isn't my boyfriend. He's just a nice man who is allowing me to stay at his place for a few days." She raised her chin as if defying Mary to say anything else about the relationship with Daniel.

Cameron released a tired sigh. "The other places you've been in your travels... Anyone give you problems? Can you think of anyone who might have been angry enough with you to want to harm you?"

"I try not to make enemies wherever I go. I can't think of anyone like that. Trust me, if I thought of anyone I'd tell you."

"I just thought you might have thought of somebody since the last time I questioned you," he replied.

She shook her head with an edge of her own frustration. "I just wish I could have turned my head enough to see who it was, or at least felt something that might identify the person. Thank God Courtney stepped outside when she did."

"She seems to have settled in okay at the motel," Mary said. "I have Rusty out in his cabin, but I'm not putting any other women out there until Candy's killer is behind bars."

"I'd like to think that if Kevin was responsible for Candy's murder there are no other women in town who are at risk." Cameron looked back at Lizzy. "Except the attack on you confuses everything."

"Go home, Lizzy," Mary said with a glance at her watch. "Rusty and I can finish up for the night."

"Do you mind if I take an apple?" Lizzy asked. "I

want to cut it up in slices to feed to one of Daniel's horses."

"You know that's not a problem. Go get your apple," Mary replied.

Lizzy left the counter and headed for the kitchen, where Rusty was scraping off the grill. Rusty was a big man, with copper-colored hair and ice-blue eyes. He wasn't an unfriendly man, but he wasn't particularly sociable, either.

"Hey, Rusty, I'm just going to grab an apple and slice it real quick," she said.

"Whatever," he replied, not turning from the grill.

She stepped into the walk-in refrigeration unit and grabbed one of the apples from a bin, then stepped back out and grabbed a knife.

As she sliced the apple into small sections she slid a glance toward Rusty. He was about the right height to be her attacker and his arms were big, like the one that had wrapped around her neck.

But she and Rusty had never exchanged a cross word with each other, and he certainly wouldn't see her as a threat to his job. She had no desire to be a cook. It just didn't make sense that he would want her to leave town.

As she placed the apple slices into a small baggie, she realized it would be easy for her to speculate and see bogeymen everywhere in Grady Gulch. There were a hundred men who were about the same height as Rusty, and each of them was a rancher and had firm arm muscles. Picking out her attacker from the group of men who had potential was like finding a needle in the proverbial haystack.

"Good night, Rusty," she said as she grabbed her baggie.

"See ya later," he replied as she left the kitchen.

As she walked back into the dining area, Cameron stood. "I'm heading out, too. I'll walk you to your car, Lizzy. Good night, Mary. I'll see you sometime tomorrow."

"Try to get some sleep, Cameron," Mary called after him.

"I'll do my best," he replied, and then he and Lizzy stepped out the front door.

The air was warm and the night still except for the sound of their footsteps as they walked to her car in the parking lot. "Not that it's any of my business, but what's the deal between you and Mary?" she asked when they'd reached her driver door.

"There is no deal between us except friendship." His frustration was obvious in his voice. "I admire her tremendously and I think she's stunning, but anytime I try to let her know I might be interested in pursuing anything with her, she turns off and shuts me out."

He shrugged his broad shoulders. "Guess I'm just not her type. You'd think after all this time I'd just give up, but sometimes she looks at me in a way that gives me just enough hope to be patient. Matters of the heart just seem damned complicated to me."

Lizzy smiled. "I don't stay in one place long enough to have matters of the heart." She opened her car door. "Thanks for walking with me, and like Mary said, go home and get some sleep."

"That's exactly where I'm headed." He raised a

hand in goodbye as she closed her door and started her engine.

She pulled out of the café parking lot and headed in the direction of Daniel's home. Matters of the heart. This was the first time in her life she thought her heart might be more involved than it should be with somebody. And that was a bad thing.

She'd only hoped to pull some of the sadness out of Daniel's eyes on that first night when she'd sat across from him in his booth. She hadn't expected the smoky sexiness his gaze held sometimes when he looked at her. She hadn't expected the tenderness in his touch, the protectiveness that surged up inside him at unexpected times where she was concerned.

Mary had warned her not to break his heart, but Lizzy feared that's exactly what was going to happen if she didn't distance herself from him.

Making love with him had been a huge, wonderful, magical mistake. Even now, seated in her car as she thought about being with him, her body warmed and desire cascaded through her and she wanted to be in his arms once again.

She couldn't let it happen again. She had to mentally and emotionally keep the distance from him that she needed so that when it was time to move on she could do so without looking back.

Still, as she pulled into the long driveway that led to Daniel's house and saw the front porch light burning bright against the darkness of the night, it felt curiously like coming home.

She got out of the car, grabbed her bag of apple slices

off the passenger seat and, instead of heading straight into the house, walked toward the barn, where she knew Molly was stabled.

It was a gorgeous night with the moon nearly full overhead and stars glittering like jewels in the sky. She felt a serenity of spirit as she listened to a slight breeze rustle through the leaves of the nearby trees, smelled the sweet green pasture grass and anticipated seeing the gentle mare once again.

When she pulled open the barn door, the utter darkness inside the building greeted her. Knowing there had to be a light someplace nearby, she ran her hand along the interior wall and found a switch. When she pushed it up, bright lights illuminated the barn.

The building was huge and the area where she stood held a variety of farm equipment. At the other end of the barn she could see the horse stalls, hear the soft whinnies of the animals.

She headed to that end of the barn, a layer of straw beneath her feet muffling the sound of her footsteps. It smelled like a wonderful blend of horse and hay and leather.

"Molly?" she said softly as she approached the stalls. "Molly, I brought you a little treat."

The first stall she passed was Dandy's, and she couldn't help but remember how magnificent Daniel had looked on the horse's back. The second and third stalls held horses she'd seen in the corral but didn't know by name. Molly was in the last enclosure and greeted Lizzy with a soft nicker.

"Hey, pretty girl. We're going for a ride in the morning, so I thought I'd bring you a little treat. I figure it's always good to bribe a big animal when you intend to ride on their back."

She pulled one of the apple slices out of the baggie and held it out to Molly, who took it from her with a gentle nibble of her lips. "You're such a sweetheart," Lizzy said as she pulled another slice from the bag.

She felt almost guilty giving Molly the apple and not the other horses, but she wasn't sure of the others' temperament and she wasn't going to ride any of them the next morning.

She had just given Molly the last slice of apple when the lights in the barn went off, plunging her into complete darkness.

Her heart lurched and a nervous laugh escaped her lips. "Daniel? Is that you?"

She stood frozen in place and waited for a reply, but none was forthcoming. "Come on, this isn't funny. Turn the lights back on. I was just giving Molly some apple slices."

Fear suddenly tightened her chest as she sensed somebody moving toward her in the darkness. "Daniel?" She whispered his name hoarsely as her throat constricted. "Daniel, is that you?"

There was no answer, no deep laughter to let her know he was playing a joke on her. "Hello? Who's there?"

She felt the person getting closer, heard the sound of deep breathing. "I warned you. You should have listened to me." The familiar guttural voice came from far too close to her and shot instant terror through her.

"Why are you doing this? What did I do to you?" Her mind frantically tried to recall what she'd seen before the lights had gone out. But, before she could do anything, she was shoved hard enough that she slammed down to the ground on her hands and knees.

She didn't have a chance to scream as a vicious kick to her stomach whooshed the air from her lungs and she collapsed to the floor. She couldn't breathe. She couldn't get enough air to scream for help. In the back of her mind she knew she was in terrible danger, but she couldn't move and the kicks began in earnest.

He kicked her ribs, her arms and legs. Sobbing with pain and shock she tried to crawl away, but she couldn't get away from his foot, from the pain of each blow. A scream was stuck in her head, but she couldn't find the air to allow it to release into the night.

She was going to die there in Daniel's barn and she wouldn't know who killed her, she wouldn't know why he wanted her dead. And then she couldn't think anymore because there was nothing but the pain, terrible, agonizing pain.

She almost welcomed the kick to her head as it dulled her senses and brought heavy shadows into her consciousness. She welcomed the darkness, and when he kicked her again in the head, everything went black.

Chapter 9

Daniel saw her car drive in. He watched in confusion as she left the car and headed toward the barn, then remembered he told her that Molly would love some pieces of apple. She must have brought some with her from the café. He watched until the barn light came on and then moved back to the sofa and turned up the volume on the television.

He didn't want her to think he'd just been standing at the front door, eagerly awaiting her return, even though that's exactly what he'd been doing.

The weather report was on and he watched the weekly forecast, disappointed that the report mentioned nothing about the possibility of rain. The crops could use a nice gentle rain.

He was halfway through the sports report when he realized Lizzy should have been inside by now. It shouldn't take that long to feed Molly a couple of pieces of apple. He got up and walked to the front door and saw that the barn light was now off.

So, where was Lizzy? He didn't see her approaching the house. Her car was empty. His heart thrummed a slight rhythm of sudden stress.

What had happened to Lizzy?

He stepped out the front door and listened to see if he could hear her. Nothing. The warm night held nothing but the ordinary sounds of home. Tree leaves rustled in a slight breeze, and insects clicked and chattered their nightly song. There was no sound that didn't belong to the June night.

"Lizzy?" He called her name as he fought the sense of panic that tried to take hold of him. "Lizzy, where are you?"

When he heard no reply, the panic flared higher. He'd watched her go to the barn, and so that's where he headed. Maybe she'd tripped over something, hurt her leg and now couldn't get back to the house. But, that didn't explain the lights inside being off or the fact that she hadn't answered his call.

The hotter his panic flared the faster he walked, until he broke into a run. When he reached the barn he turned on the lights, and at the far end of the interior he saw her.

"Lizzy!" he cried as his heart crashed with a sickening bang against his ribs. He raced to her, and when he reached her he feared she was dead. She was curled into a fetal ball, but where her T-shirt rode up on her side he saw the dark, ugly bruises beginning to form. The side of her face was also darkening.

"No…no!" He fell to his knees at her side and felt for a pulse. Was it there? He frantically moved his fingers along the curve of her jaw, along the soft skin of her neck, seeking a pulse of life.

When he felt it, he nearly cried with relief. Thank God. She was alive but unconscious and needed immediate medical attention.

He rose to his feet, torn between leaving her there all alone and his need to get to a phone. He knew it might be dangerous for him to try to move her, so he turned and raced out of the barn and toward the house.

He fought against the sickening emotion that threatened to overwhelm him. What had happened? What the hell had happened in the barn? Had one of the horses somehow gotten out of the stall and kicked her? Half trampled her to death? It was the only thing that made any kind of sense, and yet he couldn't imagine any of his horses attacking her.

As he raced into the house, he grabbed his cell phone from the coffee table and punched in the emergency numbers. "This is Daniel Jefferson. I need an ambulance right now at my place." He quickly gave his address, pocketed his cell phone and then raced back to the barn.

Lizzy hadn't moved, and a quick glance around let him know the horses were all still securely stabled. So what had happened inside here? What had happened to Lizzy?

He sank down next to her, still afraid to touch her in case he caused further damage. "Lizzy, honey, can you wake up now?" His chest constricted with a tightness that left him half-breathless. "Lizzy, I need you to wake up and talk to me. Please, honey. Just open your eyes. Just let me see those gorgeous eyes for a minute."

He couldn't lose her, not now, not this way. Once again he almost cried in relief as he heard the sound of a distant siren growing closer. Help was coming, and somehow, someway, they had to make her okay.

He left her side again only to rush back out into the night and direct the ambulance to the barn. "She's in the barn. I don't know what happened to her," he said as the two paramedics pulled a gurney from the back of the vehicle.

Before they got into the barn, a second official car pulled up. Cameron jumped out of the driver door and hurried toward Daniel. "I heard the call for an ambulance needed out here and figured I'd better check it out."

"It's Lizzy. Something happened to her. At first I thought maybe one of the horses had kicked her or trampled her, but they're all secured and there's no way it could have been one of them. She got home from work okay and then she went into the barn. Something happened, but I don't know what." Daniel was vaguely aware that he was rambling as he and Cameron followed the paramedics into the barn.

Cameron gripped his arm to hold him back so the medical team could work without his hovering. "Talk to me, Daniel. Tell me what you know."

I know that I will be destroyed if she doesn't make it through this. I know that somehow she is in my heart more than my wife ever was, more than anyone could ever be. These thoughts slithered through Daniel's brain, but of course he didn't speak them aloud.

"I don't know much," he replied. He explained about watching Lizzy pull up and walk to the barn, about his assumption that she probably had apple slices to feed to one of the horses.

"She did. I was at the café when she asked Mary if she could take an apple."

Daniel nodded. "So I watched her go into the barn, saw the light go on, and then I went back to the sofa to watch the weather report, assuming she'd be in at any moment. After a while I realized it felt like she'd been gone too long, so I went to look for her."

He looked over to where the paramedics had loaded her onto the gurney. "That's where I found her, and I immediately called for help."

He and Cameron backed out of the barn as the paramedics rolled Lizzy out and toward the waiting ambulance. "I need to get my keys from the house," Daniel said.

"I'll meet you at the hospital," Cameron replied as Daniel took off running toward the house.

It was a dream, he thought as he hurried inside to grab his keys. It was a horrendous, heart-screaming nightmare, and he just wanted to wake up and see Lizzy walking through his front door, talking about the people she'd waited on that night.

With keys in hand he ran to his truck. Both the ambulance and Cameron's car had already left. Daniel jumped into his truck, his mind whirling as sharp pains pierced his heart.

Somebody must have attacked her. Somebody had sneaked up on her in the barn and beaten the hell out of her. He clenched the steering wheel so tight his fingers went numb.

Who? It made sense that it was probably the same person who had attacked her before, but who in the hell was it and why was he after Lizzy?

Lizzy. His heart cried her name as he pressed on the gas pedal, exceeding the speed limit to get to the hospital as quickly as possible. She had to pull through this, but as he thought about how still she'd been, how pale and small she'd looked, his entire body shuddered with dread.

His hands relaxed as the sight of the hospital came into view. Grady Gulch Memorial Hospital was small but staffed with good doctors and nurses.

He parked and raced for the emergency room entrance, his heart still hammering hard and fast. Cameron was already standing in the waiting room. "They've taken her back to get her checked out. I imagine it's going to be a while before we hear anything." He gestured toward the chairs. "Why don't you sit and I'll get us a cup of coffee from the machine."

"None for me," Daniel said as he sank into one of the chairs. He felt that if he tried to put anything into his stomach right now, it just might not stay down.

Cameron returned with a foam cup of coffee in hand and sat next to Daniel with a tired sigh. "What are you thinking?" he asked.

Daniel stared down at the tiled floor. "I'm thinking I wish I hadn't watched the weather report. I'm thinking that when I saw her headed for the barn I should have gone out and joined her. Dammit, I should have been there in the barn with her." He raised his gaze to meet Cameron's. "And I'm thinking that whoever attacked her the first time and told her to leave town was pissed because she hadn't done what he'd told her to do, and tonight he found her again."

"Who in the hell could it be?" Cameron asked.

"Aren't I supposed to be the one asking *you* that question?" Daniel said wryly.

Cameron sighed again. "I've never felt so impotent as sheriff. My number one goal has always been the safety of the people of Grady Gulch, and now I have one young woman murdered and another apparently beaten to within an inch of her life. I called for a couple of my deputies to head out to your barn and see if the attacker left anything of himself behind. We'll wait until morning light and check for car tracks or whatever else we can find in the general area. Whoever was in that barn didn't walk to your place from town. If we can find some tire tracks, I'll cast them and compare them to every vehicle in the whole town."

"Just find him, Cameron."

"I'm doing my best." He took a sip of his coffee and then continued, "Lizzy told me a couple of days ago that she was getting ready to move on from Grady Gulch. Maybe it's time she did that, if nothing else for her own safety."

Daniel's heart rebelled at the very thought, and yet deep in his soul he knew that it had always been Lizzy's intention to move on. Besides, how could he ask her to stay someplace where her life might be at risk? "Maybe you're right," he finally said around the hollow ache of his heart.

The two of them fell silent then as they waited to hear if the entire conversation had been moot because Lizzy wasn't going to pull through.

There was nothing worse than waiting to hear about the condition of a loved one, Daniel thought. Minutes felt like hours, and he could only sit and think about all the terrible things that might be happening behind the closed doors ahead of them.

As he thought of those dark bruises he'd seen on her, he felt her pain, a jagged piercing ache that shot him to his feet to begin a pace of impatience.

Cameron got up for a second cup of coffee as Daniel continued pacing back and forth in the small room. What was taking so long? Why hadn't the doctor come out to tell them something?

It was another half an hour before Dr. Michael Lawrence finally walked out the door to greet them. "She's stable," he began, and the words nearly cast Daniel to his knees in relief. "But, she's still unconscious. All our tests have indicated there's no brain swelling, although it's obvious she was kicked several times in the head. She has a couple of cracked ribs and bruises pretty much from head to toe. All of them appear to be the result of her being kicked over and over again." He frowned. "Somebody wanted her badly hurt or dead. One more kick to her head and I have a feeling we wouldn't be having this conversation."

"But, she's going to be all right?" Daniel asked.

Dr. Lawrence frowned. "I'm not happy that she hasn't regained consciousness yet, but I think she's going to be okay. It's going to take her some time to get back on her feet. She took one hell of a beating."

"Can I see her?"

"Can I keep you from it?" Dr. Lawrence asked with a small smile.

"Not unless you have a big gun," Daniel replied.

"Room 119."

Daniel left Cameron and the doctor and burst through the door to find her room. The hallway smelled of some sort of pine cleaner and antiseptic soap.

The last time he'd been there was the night that Janice and Cherry had died. The city morgue was in the basement of the building. He never wanted to go to the basement again.

When he found the room he sought, he entered to see Lizzy looking small and fragile against the big hospital bed. She'd been placed in a hospital gown and one arm was out of the blanket that covered her.

The sight of that small arm, dark with bruises, made him half-crazy with rage and sorrow and guilt. He pulled a chair up next to the bed and sank down and stared at her face.

He loved her face, even though half of it was showing the signs of the deep purple bruises to come. Why hadn't she regained consciousness? Had the doctor missed something?

He leaned forward. "Lizzy? Honey, I know you're in there somewhere. You need to come back. You need to wake up."

There was no response, not even a faint flicker of an eyelid or a change in her slow, even breathing. Would she ever wake up? And if she did, was there going to be any kind of residual damage?

One thing was clear. She was going to need somebody to help her in her recuperation process, and he was committed to being that person.

He leaned back in the chair and released a weary sigh. He would do whatever it took to get Lizzy back to health, and then he would have to tell her goodbye.

She rose up from the darkness just enough to be aware of faint voices and pain. She couldn't make out what the voices were saying, but the pain shouted loud, hitting her in every area of her body.

She tried to fight past it, to open her eyes and see what was going on, but the pain was too great, the confusion in her head too tumbled, and instead she eagerly embraced the darkness as it rose up to claim her once again.

The next time the darkness began to clear she became aware of more things: the feel of the bed beneath her and the hospital scent in the air. Why was she in a hospital? Had she been in a car accident? She remembered leaving the café, Cameron walking her out to her car. What? What had happened after that?

The barn. The apple. She should be in the barn with Molly. As the memory of what had taken place in the barn pierced through the veil of darkness, a cry escaped her lips and full consciousness slammed into her.

"Lizzy?"

Daniel's voice came from someplace at her side, and she slowly turned her head to see him seated in a chair next to her. He looked like a wild man, his curly hair standing on end and his eyes dark and filled with such torment she wanted to weep for him.

"I'm okay," she said, hoping those simple words would take away some of the darkness in his eyes. She glanced past him toward the window, where the early light of day was streaking across the sky. "Long night, huh?"

He raked a hand through his hair, letting her know exactly how it had come to be in its current position. "You have no idea. I need to go get the doctor and let him know that you're awake. Will you be okay while I'm gone?"

She forced a pained smile. "I'll be fine, and I'm certainly not going anywhere."

He got up from the chair and raced for the door. It was only as he disappeared from her sight that her smile fell and tears burned at her eyes. Everything hurt. Even drawing a deep breath created a wealth of pain inside her.

As she tried to sit up, she was struck by a wave of dizziness that instantly forced her back to a prone position. He tried to kill her, she thought with a touch of horror. He'd almost kicked her to death. What kind of a man did that to a woman? To anyone? It had been an act of sheer brutality, of evil hatred.

Daniel returned with a white-haired man he introduced as Dr. Michael Lawrence. "Well, young lady, it's good to see you finally awake," the doctor said as he moved to the side of her bed. "You were beginning to worry me. How are you feeling?"

"Like I've had a close encounter with a very big truck," she replied.

"I'd love to have the name of that big truck," Cameron said from the doorway. His khaki uniform was a wrinkled mess, as if he'd slept in it all night long.

"I wish I could give you a name," Lizzy replied.

"Right now I want both of you out of here so I can have a little time with my patient," Dr. Lawrence said firmly.

A few minutes and a couple of prods and pokes later, Dr. Lawrence stepped back from her. "You have three cracked ribs, bruising on both sides and on your arms and legs. You will probably feel the residual effects of a concussion."

"Great. When can I get out of here?"

"I'd like to keep you overnight for observation," he began.

"I've already been here overnight. I don't want to stay another one."

He frowned and was silent for a long moment. "You're going back to Daniel's house?" She nodded. "I'll tell you what, let's see how you get through today. If you can get mobile without too much dizziness or nausea then I'll make the call about releasing you later today."

"Sounds fair," she replied, making a conscious decision not to mention that just trying to sit up had made her nauseous and dizzy.

"I know Sheriff Evans has been waiting to speak with

you, and Daniel has been beside himself with worry, so I'll let the two of them back in if you feel up to it."

All she really wanted was to get out of there and back to Daniel's house. She wanted to sink into the bed in his guest room and sleep until her pain was gone.

The doctor left the room and Daniel and Cameron bumped shoulders as they unconsciously fought to get into the room first. She might have laughed if she hadn't been aware of how badly laughing would hurt.

For the next half an hour Cameron questioned her, making her go over and over the event in the barn in the hopes that she might have seen something, sensed something before the lights had gone out and during her attack.

"I'm sorry, Sheriff, I didn't see anyone but Molly before the lights went out and that barn was pitch-black when he went berserk on me." She closed her eyes as the memory shot a deep shudder through her.

A warm hand covered hers and she opened her eyes to Daniel. The caring in his eyes surged a new strength through her. "I just don't have any information that will help you," she whispered.

Daniel squeezed her hand and returned to the chair next to the bed. "I'm going to head back out to Daniel's place now that it's daylight and see what we can find," Cameron said.

"And you're going with him," Lizzy said to Daniel. "I don't want you spending the day here when you have horses to care for and chickens to feed and crops to… crops and chores that need to be done."

"But…" he began.

"Please, Daniel, go home," she interrupted him. "I plan on spending most of the day sleeping. There's absolutely no reason for you to stay here." She didn't want him to witness her pain, and she didn't have the strength to pretend that she didn't hurt.

Daniel looked at Cameron. "If I head home, will you post a guard?"

"I was going to do that anyway. I've got Ben Temple on his way," Cameron replied.

Lizzy stared at first one man and then the other. It hadn't occurred to her that she might still be in danger, but she suddenly realized that if the man in the barn had meant to kill her, then he hadn't accomplished his goal. And that meant he might try again.

"Lizzy, nobody is ever going to hurt you again," Daniel exclaimed. "When you get back to my place, I promise you that nobody will get close enough to you to do any harm again."

"And I'm determined to overturn every rock in this town to find this creep," Cameron said.

At that moment Deputy Ben Temple stepped into the room. "Hey, Lizzy, how are you doing?" he asked.

"It's not my best day," she replied.

"Well, you don't have to worry. I'm going to be sitting on a chair just outside your door until you leave here, and trust me, nobody is going to get by me unless it's Daniel, Cameron or Dr. Lawrence. Oh, and whatever nurse is on duty."

"Thanks, Ben. I appreciate it." Suddenly she was exhausted.

"Okay, everybody out, and let's let Lizzy get some rest," Cameron said.

Minutes later Lizzy was alone in the room, and when a nurse whose name tag said Cheryl came in and offered pain medication, Lizzy eagerly accepted. She was a strong woman, but she wasn't a silly martyr and if there was a shot or a pill that would take away some of her pain, that would relax her into sleep, she was so there.

She slept until noon, when they delivered lunch to her room. Although every movement brought pain, she also realized she was hungry, and as far as she was concerned that was a good sign.

She finished lunch and then for the first time got out of bed. She managed to wobble her way into the bathroom, and when she looked into the mirror she gasped. One side of her face was a deep purple, and when she pulled up the hospital gown to look at her body she realized why she hurt. Her ribs and thighs were deeply colored with bruising. He'd really done a number on her.

Still, she'd survived, and she'd not only survived but she was actually standing. And she was still standing thirty minutes later when Dr. Lawrence stopped in to check on her.

"So, you're up and about," he said. "How do you feel?"

"Stiff…sore, but the dizziness I woke up with is gone and I'm feeling stronger." She realized at that moment how desperately she wanted to get out of there, how desperately she wanted to be at Daniel's house. She wanted the comfort of him and his home that had become familiar to her.

"Any dizziness or blurred vision?"

"No, nothing like that. My head feels okay. It's just all the bruising that hurts, and it hurts to breathe too deep. But, I'm still ready to get out of here."

Dr. Lawrence studied her for a long moment. "If you were going anywhere but Daniel's I would insist that you stay here. But, Daniel has called me four times today to check in on you. He sat in that chair all night long waiting for you to open your eyes. I feel confident that I'm placing you in capable hands, so I'll let him know I'm releasing you."

"Thank you," she said simply.

As he left the room she walked to the window and stared outside. The horror of the attack still simmered in her, but as she thought of going home with Daniel some of the horror ebbed away.

And that scared her. She'd never had a place that felt like home, at least not since she'd left her mother's house at the age of eighteen. Certainly her apartment in Chicago hadn't been a true home. It had just been a place to shower and sleep after long hours on the job.

In the last four months of her journey through her bucket list she hadn't found any place that had tempted her to stay, and yet Daniel's place felt oddly like home.

As she turned from the window and felt the pain that walked with her back to the bed, she realized what she should be focused on was getting well enough to pack her bags and get out of town.

She'd been warned to leave town once with an arm squeezing against her throat and nearly beaten to death because she hadn't heeded the warning.

It had never been her intention to stay here, and her feelings for Daniel couldn't change her mind. She would take a few days to heal, and after that she'd be ready to put Grady Gulch and painful attacks and Daniel Jefferson behind her.

Chapter 10

"You want some more soup?" Daniel asked Lizzy as he entered the guest bedroom, where she lay in the bed. In the past three days since he'd brought her home from the hospital, he'd insisted she stay in bed as he waited on her hand and foot.

"No thanks," she said, a touch of irritability in her voice. "What I want is to get out of this bed."

He pulled up the chair next to her bed. "But, you know that Doc Lawrence said that the best medicine for you right now is bed rest."

"Yeah, but I think I might be getting bedsores," she replied.

Daniel laughed. "I don't think you're in any danger of that. You've been up and down quite a few times to sit with visitors."

Her features relaxed into a small smile. "Honestly, I've been so surprised by having so many people come by."

"People care, Lizzy. People here care about you." He studied her face, pleased that the bruising on her cheek had turned the yellow of healing.

"Don't listen to me. I'm just being a brat," she finally replied. "You've been so kind to me, and here I am complaining."

He smiled. "You're just getting a little housebound crazy. You want to play a couple of games of gin rummy?"

"I'm really pretty sick of beating your butt every day at card games," she said with a wicked little smile.

"I think you cheat. It's the only thing to explain the losing streak I've been on for the past couple of days." His eyes twinkled teasingly.

"I think even if we played Old Maid, you'd wind up being her," she replied with a smile. The smile faded and she looked at him with curiosity. "Tell me about your marriage."

The question came out of left field and instantly tightened the muscles in his stomach. "What do you want to know about it?"

"Tell me about Janice. You never talk about her. You rarely even mention her name."

"She was beautiful and vibrant and very social. She loved eating out at the café and going down to The Corral and dancing the night away." He chose his words carefully, unwilling to malign the dead as the old familiar guilt welled up inside him.

"Your marriage must have been wonderful," Lizzy said softly.

He stared at her. Wonderful? Not hardly. "Our marriage was difficult," he finally answered as surprise flickered across Lizzy's features. "Janice was five years younger than me, and I think at the time we got married Janice wanted to be a bride but she didn't really have any interest in being a wife. She spent so much time with Cherry and Maddy there were times I felt like I married all three women. She hated the ranch, she hated her life here, and I think at the very end she hated me." He frowned, realizing he'd said far too much more than he'd initially intended.

Lizzy stared at him for a long moment, as if digesting what he'd just spilled out. "What happened on the night she died?"

Daniel got up from the chair and moved to stand at the window, where he stared out unseeing as miserable memories of that final night with Janice filled his head.

"I'd promised her when we got married that every Friday night we'd go to the café for pie and coffee and every Saturday night we'd go to The Corral and have a few drinks and dance. At the time it seemed an easy promise to keep, but on that particular Saturday in the late afternoon I had a horse go down with colic. I called Fred Jenkins out to check on the animal, and he thought maybe the cause was some new grain that I'd given her that had clumped in her stomach. I was frantic. When a horse goes down, it's always a bad situation. She was a good mare and in such obvious distress. Fred and I agreed that the best thing I could do was walk the horse.

Thirty minutes walking and thirty minutes resting for however long it took to get her feeling better."

He turned from the window to once again face Lizzy, who was obviously listening with rapt attention. "I walked that mare for the next three and a half hours, until her discomfort was gone and I felt like we were over the crisis. By the time I came back into the house, it was almost seven-thirty and I was beyond exhaustion. I walked in to find Janice dressed to the nines and wearing her red high-heel dancing shoes, and I knew we were going to have a problem."

He could still remember the sound of one of her feet tapping impatiently on the floor, her lips pressed together thinly in controlled anger.

Take back the night, he thought to himself. If he could just take back that night. He doubted that he and Janice would have remained married for much longer, but at least she would have lived to find happiness someplace else.

"You didn't want to go to The Corral," Lizzy said, her voice whisper-soft.

He gave her a curt nod. "That was the very last thing I wanted to do. I was dirty and exhausted. I'd spent everything I had trying to bring that horse back from the edge. All I wanted was a hot shower and my bed. For the two years of our marriage, we'd never missed the Friday and Saturday night outings, but that night I wasn't going anywhere."

"And she got mad."

Daniel emitted a bark of bitterness. "We both got mad. She told me I was breaking a promise, and I told her she was a spoiled brat." Guilt surged up inside him once again. "We both said ugly things to each other." He raked a hand through his hair and shook his head. "I should have just sucked it up and gone to The Corral with her. If I'd done that, everything would have been fine. Instead she called Cherry to come get her, and you know how things ended."

Lizzy studied his face for a long moment. "And so it's all your fault."

He felt his jaw muscles tighten. "I should have just done what she wanted," he replied.

"And she should have been grown-up enough to recognize that you'd had a difficult day, that sometimes promises can't be met because real life gets in the way. Daniel, Janice's and Cherry's deaths weren't your fault."

He hadn't realized how badly he'd needed to hear those words from somebody, from anybody, until he heard them from her. "But, if I'd just gone with her then she never would have called Cherry, and both women would still be alive," he said, unable to let go of the weight of guilt in his chest.

"From what I heard about the accident it was snowy that night, and the ruling on the accident was not just inclement weather but also excessive speed. Were you in that car with your foot pressed down on the gas pedal? I don't think so. You weren't responsible for what happened that night, Daniel. How long do you intend to beat yourself up about something that wasn't your fault?"

He stared at her in stunned surprise, and something snapped and broke off inside him, something that alleviated the heavy weight of guilt that had been with him for so long. He sank back down in the chair next to her, and she immediately took one of his hands in hers.

"So, your Friday night pie ritual at the café wasn't about you loving your wife so much you couldn't let her go, it was an act of penance because you've felt so responsible for her death."

"For a while I felt as if everyone in town blamed me. I don't know exactly what Janice told Cherry about our fight, and I don't know how many people Cherry called before she got here to pick Janice up that night, but basically the information going around town was that I'd kicked Janice out of the house after I'd beaten her half to death."

She squeezed his hand. "Oh, Daniel, you have to let this go. You have to be happy again."

His heart swelled in his chest. "That's what you've brought back into my life, Lizzy. You've made me happy again. You've made me think about life's possibilities." God, he wanted to tell her he loved her. The words burned on the tip of his tongue with the need to be released.

"And I hope you continue on that path when I leave here."

His words of love instantly froze on his lips. He'd been foolish in allowing his heart to get involved with her. She'd made it clear from the very beginning that she had no intention of remaining in Grady Gulch, in staying with him.

"I'll keep that in mind," he said as he once again got up from the chair. He needed some distance. He grabbed the soup bowl that was on the bedside table. "You need anything?" he asked.

"No, I'm fine for now." Those whiskey eyes of hers stared at him intently as if trying to peer into his very soul.

"I've got a little surprise planned for you later, if you feel up to it."

She smiled. "Whatever it is, I'm in if it has anything to do with me getting out of this bed."

"It does. I'll tell you a little more about it later." With the soup bowl in hand he turned and left the room, a dull ache where his heart should be.

He reached the kitchen, rinsed the soup bowl and placed it into the dishwasher and then moved to the window to stare outside.

He hadn't been out of the house since Lizzy had come there from the hospital. He'd paid a man who often worked for him to come in and take care of the daily chores. Daniel didn't want to take any chances where Lizzy's safety was concerned. He intended to remain in the house until whoever had beat her up was caught or she left town.

And she was leaving town.

She'd brought him back to life, opened his heart to loving again, and soon she was going to leave town before they could fully explore a real relationship.

There were moments he was convinced she loved him back, when he'd seen something shining from her eyes that filled him with hope, with an excitement he'd never felt before. He'd felt love in her touch, in the soft smiles she gifted to him, but none of that mattered.

He hadn't been enough for his wife, and apparently he wasn't enough for Lizzy.

He'd been a fool when he'd married Janice, a fool driven by the desire to be married and start a family, blinded by lust and fantasy. And, it appeared he was a fool again for falling in love with Lizzy.

Lizzy sat on the edge of the bed and stared out the window, where the darkness of night had fallen. Daniel had been unusually quiet during the afternoon and evening, and she wondered if talking about Janice had opened old wounds.

The guilt he'd carried for so long was tragic, and she wasn't sure a simple conversation with her had done anything to really ease it. He deserved better. He deserved so much more than what he'd gotten from life, from love, thus far.

Her bruises were slowly fading and she had most of her strength back. Mary had told her when she'd come to visit the day before that her job was waiting for her whenever she was ready to come back, but Lizzy wasn't coming back. In the next two days she intended to be back on the road again, getting away from Grady Gulch…away from Daniel.

Things had gotten far too complicated here. What had begun as a simple stop on her bucket list had gone way out of control. Lizzy didn't like complicated. Easy and breezy, that's the way she liked it, with her expecting nothing from nobody and depending only on herself.

She needed to get out of Daniel's way so he could start building something meaningful, something loving and good with the woman he was meant to be with for the rest of his life.

"Ready for your surprise?" he asked as he appeared in her doorway.

"Definitely, but it's awfully late in the day for surprises."

"The later the better for this surprise," he replied with a mysterious twinkle in his eyes.

She got up from the bed, the pain in her ribs much better and the ache in her thighs barely discernible. "Okay then, lead me to it." She suddenly noticed he had a gun tucked into the waistband of his jeans. "What's that for?" she asked in surprise.

For just a moment his eyes took on a hard glint. "I told you I wouldn't let anyone hurt you again. In order to have your surprise we have to leave the house." He touched the butt of the gun. "I'm just being cautious, that's all."

"And I like that about you," she returned with a light smile.

They walked down the stairs and to the back door, and then he turned to face her. "Your surprise is in the barn. Lizzy, if you feel like you can't go back in there after what happened to you, then we'll forget the whole thing." His eyes held a soft concern that whispered tenderness in her heart.

She thought about it for a minute. "A bad person did something bad to me in the barn, but that doesn't make the barn a bad place. The barn is a good place. Molly and all the other horses are there."

His gaze of concern changed to one of admiration.

"You are an amazingly strong woman, Lizzy." He grabbed her hand and together they stepped out of the back door. He locked it behind them and then took her hand once again as they began to walk across the yard toward the barn.

She could tell as they walked that his attention wasn't solely on her, but rather on their surroundings. He gazed from right to left, a slight tension in his body as if he was ready for anything or anyone that might come out of the darkness as a threat.

When they were within about twenty feet from the structure tension started to well up inside her and she squeezed Daniel's hand tighter.

"Okay?" he asked.

"Just a little twinge of nerves," she admitted. "It's a beautiful night." She tried to focus on anything but the memory of what had happened to her the last time she had been in the barn.

"A perfect clear sky," he agreed. They reached the barn and opened the door and turned on the light.

She hesitated a moment before stepping inside, but she kept her nerves under control by focusing on the familiar scents and the sounds of the horses nickering a greeting. She started to walk in the direction of the horses, but he stopped her.

"We aren't going that way," he said. "Your surprise is up here." He pointed to a wooden ladder in the corner that led up to the hayloft.

She eyed him with curiosity. "Okay."

The ladder wasn't wide enough to allow them to go up together. "Stay right behind me," he said as they began to climb. Once they both reached the loft, he checked it as if making sure nobody else was up there, then he told her to sit on a bale of hay and he'd be back.

He raced down the ladder, and Lizzy was more curious than she'd ever been. What was up there that would be considered a surprise? All she could see were bales of hay stacked here and there.

The lights downstairs went off and sudden terror stopped her heart. "It's okay, Lizzy," he called quickly, as if he knew she'd be terrified. "I turned off the lights on purpose." A flashlight beam lit the stairs and then he was back in the loft, the beam of light a welcomed glow against the darkness.

"I don't understand," she said.

"I'm hoping you will in a minute. Here, hold this." He handed her the flashlight as he moved two bales of hay into position and retrieved a bottle of wine and two glasses from where they must have been hidden earlier. "Now, move over here next to me."

As she moved to the hay bale right next to where he sat, he popped the cork on the wine and poured them each a glass. "This is nice," she said as she took the glass from him. "Nice, but a little bit odd."

He laughed. "Hopefully you won't find it so odd in just a minute." He sobered. "You told me that one of the things on your bucket list was to sit on a mountaintop and stargaze. This isn't exactly a mountaintop, but it provides a pretty good view of the stars. Turn off the flashlight."

She did as he said and the loft was once again plunged

into complete darkness. "I hate to tell you this, Daniel, but I don't see a single star."

He reached forward and unlatched two doors she hadn't realized were right in front of her. As they swung outward she gasped at the sight of the beauty of the night sky.

It was absolute magic. The stars appeared so close she felt that if she just leaned forward a little bit she could grasp a handful of the glittering lights.

"Oh, Daniel, it's beautiful." Emotion pressed tight in her chest, emotion she didn't want to examine too closely.

She couldn't believe he'd thought of her bucket list, that he'd arranged all this specifically for her benefit. He'd given her a mountaintop right there in Grady Gulch.

She leaned against the hay bale behind her and sipped the wine, her gaze captured by the astronomical splendor before her. "Do you come up here often?" She turned to look at him, his features visible by the light of the moon.

"This is my first time. I was just thinking about your bucket list earlier today and got this idea."

"It was a wonderful idea." Although she kept her focus on the skies, she was aware of his gaze lingering on her.

"Tell me about your childhood, Lizzy. Was it a good one?"

"Good in some ways, not so good in others," she replied. "My dad wasn't terrific with the child support payments, so financially we always struggled a bit. But, my mother was a wonderful, caring woman who always made me feel safe and loved. She could make a picnic of butter sandwiches seem like an elegant five-star meal."

She took another sip of the wine as she thought about her childhood. "When it comes to my father, I was the cliché child who sat on the stoop for hours waiting for him to show up because he'd made plans to take me to the zoo or to see a movie or a hundred other things. I spent a lot of nights over the years sitting on that stoop. It took me a long time to finally catch on that he wasn't dependable, that he was never going to keep a promise made to me."

The pain of the child she had once been resonated through her soul, making her realize there was still a little wounding there that would probably never heal. It had taken her a long time to realize the problem was with him and not that there was something wrong, something bad, with her.

"I'm sorry," Daniel said simply.

"It's all right. It was a long time ago. Look, there's the Milky Way."

For the next hour they sipped wine and watched the stars, pointing out constellations they recognized and enjoying easy small talk about the people in town and ranch life in general.

They didn't discuss Candy's murder or the attacks on her. Nothing negative entered the conversation at all, and Lizzy felt more relaxed than she had since the last attack on her.

The wine bottle was nearly empty when Daniel placed an arm around her shoulder and gently pulled her closer against him. She stiffened for a moment and then gave in, relaxing into his warmth and comfort.

"It would be nice if I left here with some answers," she finally said, and she wasn't sure if she was reminding him or herself that she would be leaving town soon.

"I'd like to have those same answers." His breath was warm across her cheek and smelled of the fruity, fragrant wine they'd almost polished off. "I'd like to find the bastard who hurt you and give him a little Oklahoma justice."

"'Oklahoma justice'? Is that synonymous with getting him into a dark alley and punching his lights out?"

"Something like that," he agreed.

She had more than a little bit of a buzz from the wine, but not enough to make her silly. She just felt a warm glow, and she wasn't completely clear if it was from the alcohol or the setting or the man.

"This is probably the best mountaintop I'll ever find in the whole wide world," she said softly.

His arm tightened slightly around her shoulder. "So, you can cross that off your bucket list?"

She turned to look at him and smiled. "Yes, I think that's exactly what I will do." Her smile faltered as she saw the soft expression on his face, the familiar spark in the centers of his eyes. The glow inside her intensified as she realized he was going to kiss her.

Even though she knew it was wrong, she wanted his kiss more than anything else in the world at that moment. His lips descended on hers, and she welcomed him with parted lips of her own.

It was a kiss of sweet tenderness. Their tongues

whirled together not with wild passion but with a languid, simmering sensuality that spoke not just to her hormones, but to her very heart. And she knew at that moment that even though he didn't realize it, this was her goodbye kiss to him.

Chapter 11

"How about dinner at the café tonight?" Daniel asked Lizzy the next afternoon.

"That sounds great," she agreed. She was seated on the sofa in the living room and didn't take her gaze off the afternoon talk show she'd been watching.

She'd been distant all day, and Daniel had felt her slipping away from him with each moment that passed. He'd felt the distance the moment they'd left the hayloft the night before, and it had continued into today.

He felt a sick desperation, the scent of heartache rife in the air. She'd brought him back to life, to love, and now she was going to leave him, and there was nothing he could do to stop her.

He'd somehow hoped that by giving her the mountaintop and the stars she'd fall into his arms and profess her love for him, her need to stay there in Grady

Gulch and continue their life together. He'd fantasized that she'd tell him she didn't want to finish her bucket list anywhere but there with him.

But that hadn't happened. The kiss they'd shared had lasted only a few seconds and then she'd told him she was tired and ready to go back to the house.

Once they got back inside she'd gone to bed, and when she'd awakened that morning there had been a frightening distance in her eyes, an aloof, almost impersonal manner in the way she'd interacted with him.

He was somehow hoping that by taking her back to the café tonight she'd be reminded of all the wonderful things, all the good people she loved in Grady Gulch and all the people who loved her.

By six-thirty they were ready to leave. Lizzy looked stunning in a pair of jeans and a brown-and-gold blouse that enriched the whiskey tones of her eyes. She'd pulled her long hair up in a ponytail that accented the pretty bone structure of her face, and tiny gold earrings hung from her dainty ears.

She was a bit more animated on the drive into town, talking about all the people she hoped to see during their meal. "I need to thank Mary for the apple pie she brought by day before yesterday, and I also want to see how Courtney is doing living in the motel."

"Doesn't she have parents someplace who could help her out?" Daniel asked.

"From what she told me her parents are some kind of social muckety-mucks from Evanston, and they basically disowned her when she got pregnant."

"Wow, unbelievable in this day and age," Daniel replied. The small town of Evanston was only a thirty-minute drive from Grady Gulch. It was a shame Courtney and her young son didn't have the support of parents who lived so nearby.

"What about the father of her boy?" Daniel asked.

"Not around," Lizzy replied. "And from what Courtney has told me, she doesn't expect him to ever be a part of her life or Garrett's." She sat up straighter in her seat as he pulled into the Cowboy Café parking lot. "Oh good, it looks like Courtney is working tonight," she said as Daniel spied Courtney's beat-up car in the lot.

They parked and left Daniel's truck, and when they entered the café Lizzy was instantly greeted by dozens of people. Even George Wilton, the town curmudgeon, managed to give her what appeared to be almost a smile.

Adam and Sam Benson waved from across the room, and Courtney hugged Lizzy gingerly as if afraid to hurt her. "I'm so glad to see you up and around," she said. "Everyone has been asking about you. When I heard what happened to you, I was sick."

"You okay at the motel?" Lizzy asked her.

Courtney nodded. "We're doing fine. They've given me a good rate so I can afford to be there until I find something more permanent."

"Good," Lizzy replied.

Junior Lempke lumbered toward her, a wide childish smile on his broad face. "Hi, Lizzy."

"Hi, Junior," she replied.

Junior's gaze didn't quite meet hers as his cheeks reddened with a blush. "Hi...okay," he said and turned and went back to the table he'd been clearing.

Dana Maxwell and Shirley Cook, fellow waitresses, gathered around Lizzy as Daniel stepped back, giving the women space to greet each other and have a moment of girl talk.

Surely Lizzy felt the love in the room for her. It was so warm and vibrant in the entire place. How could she walk away from this place that had embraced her so completely? How could she walk away from him? His heart crunched at this thought.

It took at least fifteen minutes before they finally made their way to a table. He consciously steered her away from the booth that had been his place of misery and guilt. He wasn't that man anymore, and even if Lizzy left him he would never go back to being that man again.

Janice and Cherry's accident had been a tragedy, but the responsibility of that car wreck no longer weighed him down with guilt. He would always be sorry that two beautiful, vibrant women died that night, but he was done feeling responsible for all of it. The night had been a combination of flared tempers between him and Janice, but Lizzy had been right, Cherry had been driving recklessly fast, as well.

"Everyone is being so nice to me," she said to him once they were seated at a table for two.

"I told you before, Lizzy, this whole town has embraced you." He picked up the menu even though he knew the contents by heart. He was afraid at that moment if he looked at her he'd tell her that he loved her.

"I'm starving," she said. "And the Wednesday night special is always chicken fried steak and mashed potatoes with gravy. That's definitely what I'm going to have."

He closed the menu. "That sounds good to me, too."

Dana Maxwell appeared at their table, her order form in hand. "Can I start you guys off with drinks?"

"Iced tea for me," Lizzy said.

"Make that two," Daniel added.

"Be back in two shakes for the rest of your order," she said as she left the table.

"She's a nice woman," Lizzy said as she followed Dana's progress back to the counter.

"I know, I've known her all my life."

Lizzy looked back at him. "Then you know she was divorced years ago and has been alone for a long time. She has pretty hair, too, and a great sense of humor."

Daniel stared at her with narrowed eyes. "Are you trying to match-make for me, Lizzy?"

Her cheeks grew pink. "I just don't want you to go back to the man you were when I first met you. When I leave here tomorrow, I want to know that you're going to live your life to the fullest and hopefully find a woman who will make a wonderful wife for you and give you a house full of children."

"Tomorrow?" He'd stopped listening to anything else after she'd said that. His heart took a nosedive into his boots. "You're leaving tomorrow?"

Her answer was delayed by the reappearance of Dana with their drinks. "Now, what can I get you two for supper?"

"Two specials," Daniel replied, not taking his gaze off Lizzy. "Tomorrow?" he repeated when Dana had once again left with their orders. "Are you sure you're up to it?"

She nodded, looking down at her iced tea as if unwilling to meet his gaze. "It's time for me to move on. I feel fine and you've been more than wonderful, but it was never meant for me to stay here." She finally looked up at him, and in the depths of her eyes he thought he saw a wealth of regret. It was there only a moment and then gone as she once again looked down at her glass.

Daniel couldn't speak. His sorrow was too intense at the moment. Intellectually, he'd known she was going to leave town eventually, but somehow his heart had convinced him that it would never really happen, that when the time came he'd be able to talk her into staying.

And now it was going to happen so fast. Tomorrow. That single word held a depth of grief he hadn't been prepared for, hadn't armed himself against.

In less than twenty-four hours she would pack up her beautiful smiles, her sense of humor and her beloved face and take them away. She'd take her passion and her wonderful way of approaching life and pack them in her suitcases and carry them off.

"I just wasn't expecting it to be so soon," he finally managed to reply.

"If it hadn't been for this last attack, I would have already been gone." She looked up at him again, and this time her eyes held no emotion whatsoever. "If I stay any longer things will just get complicated."

Things were already complicated, and she'd be lying if she didn't realize that herself. They had become complicated the moment his lips had first met hers, the day that he'd taken her into his bed and with every moment of every day they had spent together.

It was at that moment that Daniel realized he had only one weapon left in his arsenal to make her stay, and that was the love he had for her that he'd never professed.

Would it make a difference if she knew the depth of his feelings for her? Would his love for her be enough for her to forget the promise she'd made to her dying mother? He would never know unless he let his love for her be known.

However, as he leaned forward to speak of his love, Dana arrived at the table with their orders. "Here we are, two Wednesday night specials, and it looks like Rusty got a good do on those mashed potatoes." She set the plates down in front of them. "Now, is there anything else either of you need?"

I need you to talk Lizzy into staying here in town, Daniel thought. *I need you to make her realize that we belong together.* "Thanks, but I think we're just fine," he said aloud.

"Hmm, this looks yummy," Lizzy exclaimed, obviously not having a clue as to the utter turmoil that twisted his soul.

He had to tell her that he loved her. If he let her leave there without her knowing how he felt about her, then he would be the fool who would never know what might have been.

She knew she'd shocked him when she'd told him she was leaving the next day, but what was equally shocking was the lump that had risen in the back of her throat when she'd told him.

It had never been her intention to stay. The promise to her mother burned bright in her heart. Besides, he hadn't asked her to stay. At least she now understood that it had been guilt more than grief that had kept him alone for so long, but that didn't mean he was ready to love again. Besides, she'd only borrowed him for a couple of weeks. She'd never meant to keep him.

They were both quiet as they ate the meal, as if telling him she was leaving the next day had stopped the need for any further conversation.

She would forever be grateful to him for his loving care and nurturing after the last attack. She would always be grateful to him for offering her his home as a safe haven when things had felt so scary.

He'd been her rock when for the first time in her life she'd needed one. But, it was time for her to let go, to finish what she'd begun to honor her mother.

Throughout the meal people stopped by to say hello to her, to tell her that it was good to see her up and around again and how sorry they had been to hear that she'd been hurt. Therefore the meal took longer to finish than usual.

When they were finished Dana came to check on them and Daniel ordered them each a cup of coffee, apparently in no hurry to get up and head back to the ranch.

When the coffee arrived, he cupped the mug in his hands and looked at her, his intent gaze tightening the muscles in her stomach. "I don't want you to leave, Lizzy."

Her heart squeezed tight as she saw the depth of emotion in his eyes. "But you know I have to."

He took a sip of his coffee, his gunmetal-gray eyes still focused on her over the rim of the mug. He placed his mug back on the table and leaned forward. "As we were eating I was thinking about your bucket list."

She quirked an eyebrow. "What about it?"

"You've already managed to check four things off your list right here in town. You worked in a café, met cowboys, rode a horse and stargazed from a makeshift mountaintop. I think if we got very creative, you could finish up your list right here."

He talked faster than she'd ever heard him, as if the words coming out of his mouth were too important to be delivered in his usual lazy speed.

"You said that you wanted to take some kind of dance lessons," he continued. "We can go down to The Corral on any Friday night and they give line-dancing lessons. You said you wanted to sing in Times Square. Well, Grady Gulch isn't exactly New York, but we do have a Main Street, and I'm sure you could draw quite a crowd."

"Not necessarily in a good way. You've never heard me sing," she said, reaching for humor to cover how touched she was that he'd apparently given this all a lot of thought, that he'd even remembered some of the things she'd told him were on her bucket list.

She looked out the window, in the back of her mind realizing darkness was beginning to fall and needing a moment to get her emotions back into control. She refused to be seduced by his words, by him, into doing something she might possibly regret later.

"Daniel, I think you just want me to stay because your life has changed with me, because you've once again become the man you were supposed to before Janice and Cherry died, and you're afraid what will happen when I leave." She reached across the table and covered one of his hands with hers. "But, you're going to be fine, Daniel. I just know you are."

He turned their hands over, so hers was captured by his, and his eyes glowed with that smoke that made her heart catch in her chest. "This isn't about what you've done for me or what I might have done with you. I know I'll never go back to being that miserable man I was when you first sat down across from me in the booth. I'm in love with you, Lizzy. I'm in love with you like I've never been with anyone else before."

She pulled her hand from his, stunned by his words, and equally stunned by how the force of them slammed her in the chest. She leaned back in her chair and fought the impulse to run from the café, to escape from him.

She hadn't expected this. She hadn't wanted it. Footloose and fancy-free, that's the way she rolled. She never wanted to leave damage behind, had never intended to get involved with anyone as she fulfilled her promise to her dying mother.

"I just… It's time for me to go." Panic. She felt absolute panic. "I never meant for things to get this far between us. I don't want you to be in love with me, and I don't want to love you."

"But, you do love me." His eyes were so intense she felt as if he were sucking the air from her body. "Tell me, Lizzy. Tell me that you love me."

She shook her head, somehow knowing that if she said the words aloud it would change everything, and she didn't want that. She had her plans, her path in life, and he wasn't even on her list.

"You know what I think?" he asked. "I think you love me, but you're afraid to let anyone into your life in a meaningful way."

"What are you talking about?" she asked, slightly offended by his words.

He leaned back in his chair, his gaze contemplative rather than accusing. "You're bright, you're beautiful and you're twenty-eight years old, and yet you told me you've never had anything but very brief relationships."

"I was working hard and then my mother died," she exclaimed. "There just hasn't been time for long-term relationships."

"I think that's what you've told yourself."

"Really? So, what is my problem, Dr. Daniel?" she asked with a small edge of sarcasm.

His reply was interrupted by Dana returning to the table to refill their coffee cups. "Everything okay here?" she asked, as if she sensed the screaming tension between them. "Anyone up for dessert?"

"None for me," Lizzy replied. Any appetite she might have had for something sweet had fled with their conversation, a conversation that should be taking place in the privacy of their own home.

She frowned. It wasn't their home. It was his home, and she didn't intend to make it her home ever.

"Nothing for me, Dana." Daniel smiled at the waitress.

"Maybe we should take this conversation back to your house," she said when Dana was gone.

"I think we should finish it here and now," he replied, an edge of steel in his voice. "Even though I've only known you a couple of weeks, it's been an intense couple of weeks and I think we've both shared a lot about ourselves."

"Okay, fine." He was right that even though they'd only had a relatively short amount of time together, she knew him better than she'd known any man in her life and she'd certainly shared more about herself with him than she had with any other man. "So, tell me why I have never had any long-term relationships."

"Because you're afraid."

"That's ridiculous," she scoffed. "I've taken off from my Chicago home to travel by the seat of my pants around the country. I'm trying new things almost every day. The only thing I'm afraid of is that the man who attacked me twice might find me one final time before I get out of town."

"I think that you're afraid to let any man close to you because they might be like your father. You don't let anyone get close enough to disappoint you, or let you down, or keep you waiting on a front porch stoop for hours."

She gasped, not only appalled that he would use

something she'd told him against her, but also by the small stab of truth that pierced through her heart.

She shoved the pain away, refusing to be caught up in some mumbo jumbo psychobabble about how her dad had hurt her and that was why she'd never had a real relationship before.

The pain was replaced by the warmth of her mother's face appearing in her head. *"Promise me, Lizzy. Take what money I have left and do all the things that make you happy."* And that's exactly what Lizzy had done… still planned to do.

"I promised my mother, Daniel, and I don't give my promises easily."

"Don't you think what would be most important to your mother was if you were happy? We can be happy together here, Lizzy. I feel it in my heart, in my soul." He leaned forward once again. "You can help me fill that big house with children. We can build something magical here, Lizzy. Isn't that truly what your mother would want for you?"

Too close. He was suddenly too close and his words hit too hard in her heart. She needed to get some air, to wash the heat off her face. She needed to stop this whole conversation before she made a mistake.

"I'm going to the restroom," she said as she slid out of the booth. She was shocked to feel tears burning at her eyes as she ran toward the back, where the bathrooms were located near the kitchen area.

She passed Mary, who stood at one of the booths visiting with a tableful of diners. When she reached the bathroom, she went directly into one of the three stalls and leaned weakly against the wall.

He loved her. At least he believed he did, but she wasn't convinced. She thought that he was probably confusing gratitude with love. There was no question that he'd transformed in the time they'd spent together.

His handsomeness and perhaps his sadness had drawn her to him initially, but it was his charm, his easy laughter and many other wonderful qualities that had the potential to ruin her plans.

What plans? a little voice whispered inside her head. *To wander from place to place never making any real friends, never connecting in a meaningful way to anyone?*

Is that what her mother would have really wanted for her? Lizzy was so confused, and if she looked deep inside herself she'd recognize that Daniel was right, there was a part of herself that was afraid to trust in love…in him.

Maybe he was right. When she'd met him she'd believed that he was the damaged goods, but maybe if she looked deep inside herself, she'd realize *she* was the one who was damaged. Maybe he was right and she'd really never left behind that wounded little girl who'd just wanted her daddy to be a part of her life.

One thing was certain. Now she just had to go back out there and tell him she was firm in her decision to leave Grady Gulch the next morning.

As she stepped out of the bathroom, a hand came from behind her and slapped hard against her mouth. Before she knew what was happening, she felt herself being dragged backward through the empty kitchen and out the back door.

The moment she was pulled out the door and into the darkness of night, the reality of what was happening set in and terror took hold.

She fought, first to get free and then to see whoever it was who held her so tight she couldn't get loose. He was strong enough that he had her nearly off the ground as he continued to pull her backward, making it impossible for her to see his face.

The light from the back door of the café promised salvation, but she was being dragged farther and farther away from it. Her screams were effectively muffled by the tightness of his big, strong hand over her mouth, and his other arm was wrapped around her neck in a horrifyingly familiar manner.

Suddenly she realized where he was dragging her… to the cabin she'd stayed in before Candy's murder. Why was he taking her there? Her heart beat so hard she was surprised nobody in the café could hear it.

Was this the same person who had slit Candy's throat? She knew that if he managed to get her into that dark cabin, she'd be dead.

Like Candy.

There would be no bucket list, no opportunity to thank Mary for her kindness, to say goodbye to Courtney and her other waitress friends. She would never see Daniel's face again.

She tried to fight against him, swinging her arms as hard as she could, kicking with her feet as she attempted to twist her head from side to side in an effort to dislodge his hand over her mouth.

But, no matter how she fought she couldn't get free, and with each step they got closer and closer to the cabin. *Daniel,* she screamed in her mind. *Oh, God, somebody help me.* Tears blurred her vision as he pulled her through the cabin door.

"If you scream I'll slit your throat. Do you understand me?"

The deep, snarling voice was the same one she'd heard twice before, and her blood froze.

"I said, do you understand me?"

She nodded, desperate to agree to whatever he wanted as long as he didn't hurt her. His hand dropped from her mouth but the other arm remained around her neck.

The light to the cabin blinked on and she squinted against the sudden brightness. "You're a stubborn woman, Lizzy. You should have left town that first time I told you."

This time his voice was more natural, and with shocked surprise she recognized it. What she didn't understand at all was why. He released her and she turned to face him, stunned to see that not only had he pulled the curtains at the windows closed, but that he also had a gun in his hand. There was a wildness in his eyes that screamed of instability.

"Sam? What are you doing? Why are you doing this?" The idea that Sam Benson would want to hurt her made no sense whatsoever.

"You make him happy, and he doesn't get to be

happy," Sam said, his voice deep and hoarse with barely suppressed rage. "As long as Cherry is dead, he has to be miserable like me."

Lizzy stared at him. She had racked her brain trying to figure out why anyone would want to harm her, and now she knew: she was merely a tool of torture for Daniel. Because Sam Benson didn't want Daniel to know happiness, because Sam Benson had obviously lost his mind when he'd lost his sister.

"Sam, you need to calm down," she said softly, acutely aware that the gun was pointed at the very center of her chest.

"I need you to get on the bed. You have to look just like Candy did when they found her." His eyes remained wild, but the gun in his hand never wavered.

Lizzy drew in a deep gulp of air. "You killed Candy?"

"Of course I didn't kill Candy. I didn't give a rat's behind about her," he scoffed. "I figure her boyfriend or someone else who found her complaining ways irritating killed her. But, if you die the same way, then the sheriff is going to think he's got some sort of serial killer on his hands. He'd never dream that it was me that killed you."

Nobody would think of her murder being committed by Sam anyway, she thought. "Sam, I'm leaving town tomorrow. You don't have to do this. I'll be gone by dawn."

"That's not good enough!" he screamed, the cords in his neck bulging. "I warned you twice, but you wouldn't listen to me. I can't believe a damn word you say. I see the way you look at him, and the way he looks at you. Now get on that bed before I shoot you."

A million thoughts flashed through Lizzy's head in the space of a breath. Would he really shoot her? The gun had no silencer on it. If he fired it everyone in the café would hear the noise.

If he truly wanted her murder to appear like Candy's in order to cover his tracks, then he'd want to use a knife on her, not a gun.

She certainly didn't want to make this easy for him. Her will to survive surged up inside her, along with the courage to gamble.

"Get on the damned bed," he yelled again.

A lifetime of emotions flashed through Lizzy as she raised her chin and returned his gaze. "Make me."

Chapter 12

"Thanks, Dana," Daniel said as the waitress topped off both his and Lizzy's coffees.

"No problem." She gave him a bright smile and then left him alone at the table. Daniel looked across the room toward the area of the restrooms, waiting for Lizzy to return to the table.

He supposed he should have just let her go in the morning and kept his feelings to himself. That probably would have been the kindest thing for him to do for her, to let her fulfill her promise to her mother without the baggage of his love on her shoulders.

They should have spent their last evening together without tension, without complicated matters of the heart taking away the simple pleasure of their last moments.

"Hi, Daniel," Mary greeted him as she walked up to the side of his table. "How are you doing?"

He wrapped his hands around his coffee mug. "As well as can be expected, I suppose. Did Lizzy tell you she was leaving town in the morning?"

Mary looked at him in surprise. "No, she didn't." A trace of sadness darkened her blue eyes. "I shouldn't be surprised, but I had been hoping…" she allowed her voice to trail off.

"Yeah, me, too."

Mary placed a gentle hand on his shoulder, as if knowing exactly what he felt at the moment. "I warned her, Daniel. I told her you were a good man and that she shouldn't break your heart."

He gave Mary a wry smile. "She didn't mean to. She just couldn't help it. She warned me from the first time she spoke that Grady Gulch was just a temporary stop."

Mary looked around the restaurant. "Where is she now?"

"We were kind of having an intense discussion and she excused herself to go to the restroom." Daniel frowned. "But, it seems like she's been gone an unusually long time."

"You want me to check on her?" Mary asked.

"Do you mind?" He suddenly felt a bit uncomfortable with the length of time she'd been gone. He knew women could spend a lot of time primping and posturing in front of a mirror, but Lizzy just wasn't that type.

"I'll be right back," Mary said and turned to head in the direction of the restrooms.

Daniel watched as she wound her way through the

tables, occasionally stopped by a patron to ask a question or to say hello.

Surely Lizzy hadn't sneaked out the back door and found a ride back to his place, unwilling to have any further conversation with Daniel.

He mentally shook his head. No, she wouldn't do that to him. She'd see this to the end, drive home with him tonight and then tell him goodbye in the morning. She wouldn't hide from that final goodbye. She just wasn't that kind of woman.

The slight edge of tension inside him increased as he saw Mary disappear down the hall to the bathroom and a moment later reappear with a worried frown creasing her forehead.

He stood as she reached his table. "She wasn't in there, Daniel. I checked the kitchen, too. She doesn't seem to be anywhere in the café."

She wouldn't have just left, not this way. He felt it in his gut. He knew her too well to believe that. "I'm going to check it out," he said to Mary.

"Should I call Cameron?" she asked, her lower lip trembling with concern.

Daniel hesitated. If Lizzy had just stepped outside for a moment because she'd needed a breath of fresh air, a little break from the conversation they were having, then calling the sheriff would be a foolish waste of his time.

But, if Lizzy had stepped outside for some air and somebody had grabbed her, her attacker had carried her off, then he wanted not just the sheriff but every deputy in town looking for her. He'd rather be foolish than be forever sorry.

"Yeah, call Cameron. I'm going to check outside." Daniel headed for the front door, attempting desperately to hold on to his simmering panic, to not allow it to release unless absolutely necessary.

Maybe she'd gone to his truck. They'd finished their meal. Maybe she'd decided to just wait in the truck until he finished his coffee and paid for their dinner.

Even as he ran to the side of his truck, he knew she wouldn't be there. Lizzy wouldn't sit in the truck and pout because he'd told her a hard truth that he believed about her.

Frantically he looked around the parking lot, seeking any sign of her. But, he couldn't find her. He couldn't find her anywhere, and the panic that he'd been trying desperately to control surged up inside him, leaving him half-breathless.

Had she stepped outside and right into danger? Was this just another repeat of what had happened with Janice? He'd told her some hard truths about herself that night, and his words had sent her out the door and to her death.

Lizzy! Her name screamed in his head as he left the parking lot and raced around the left side of the café building. If she'd stepped outside it had been through the kitchen door because he hadn't seen her return to the dining area after going to the bathroom.

Yes, that was it, she was probably standing outside the back door where the kitchen light spilled out into the night and Rusty or Junior were only a shout away.

The side of the building seemed longer than normal as he ran, hoping, praying that when he turned the corner to the back of the café he'd see Lizzy standing there. Oh, God, he wanted that. He'd gladly let her go tomorrow if she was just okay right now.

He whirled around to the back of the café and saw nothing except a stack of trash cans and the light spilling out of the kitchen.

No Lizzy.

He raced into the kitchen, where Rusty was at the grill. "Did somebody come through here? Did you see Lizzy a few minutes ago come this way?"

"Somebody came through a few minutes ago, but I was in the walk-in refrigerator and didn't see who it was."

Daniel didn't wait to hear anymore. He felt it in his gut. Lizzy had come through here, she'd stepped outside and then something had happened. But what?

Once again he darted out the door and paused, his gaze sweeping the area for any sign of her or of what might have happened.

The cabins were dark. Only Rusty's had a light shining out the window. Candy's cabin still had a stripe of crime scene tape stuck to the door, the bright yellow band tightening the muscles in Daniel's gut.

He listened, but all he could hear was the sound of diners inside and the noise that Rusty made as he threw something on the grill that popped and sizzled.

And then he saw it…a sliver of light in the window of the cabin that had been Lizzy's. Had she forgotten something and gone in to retrieve it before leaving town tomorrow? Surely if she'd remembered something she'd left behind she would have asked Daniel to go with her into the cabin.

Lizzy wasn't a foolish woman, and after the attack in the barn she'd know better than to go anywhere in the dark alone. A cold calm swept through him as he reached down and grabbed his gun from his boot.

Mary had no more tolerance for guns at dinner than she did for hats, but Daniel hadn't been about to have an outing with Lizzy without the weapon.

The gun felt weighty, slightly alien in his hand. He kept it at the ranch for protection and knew he was a proficient shot, but he certainly wasn't intimately familiar with the weapon. Still, he could easily point it at somebody and pull the trigger if it was a matter of life and death for Lizzy.

He felt as if the night around him fell away as he focused solely on the cabin ahead of him and the faint sliver of light that leaked out of a slit in the curtains.

If she was in there he just had to hope he wasn't too late to save her. If she was in there he hoped he could open the door and see her crawling around on the ground looking for a lost earring or a missing lipstick.

But, he knew she was in there, and he knew in his very gut that she was not alone. As he drew closer... closer still, his gut instinct proved right. He could hear the faint sound of voices coming from inside.

He moved even closer, hoping he could hear what was being said over the frantic pounding of his heart. "If you're going to shoot me, then just do it!" The sound of Lizzy's voice filled his very soul.

She was alive, but whoever was in there with her had

a gun. That made whoever it was and Daniel even in the weapons department. The only additional weapon Daniel had on his side was the element of surprise.

As he moved to stand in front of the door, he hoped that was enough. Summoning all the strength he possessed, he kicked the door open and burst inside.

As Lizzy's attention shot to the door that had exploded inward, Sam managed to grab her and place the knife at her throat.

As Daniel froze and stared at the two of them, Lizzy realized that there was nothing quite so cold in the entire world as the blade of a knife held against your throat. The cold seemed to seep downward, and she forced against a tremble, afraid that the slightest movement would allow the knife to cut her skin.

She saw the stunned surprise in Daniel's eyes as he lowered the gun he held just a bit. "Sam, what's going on?" His voice was low and steady, as if he recognized the madness in Sam's eyes and didn't want to feed into it in any way.

"You should know what's going on!" Sam screamed, and Lizzy could feel his body vibrating with rage, with loss and with the aching need for revenge. "You don't get to be happy, Daniel. Your actions killed my sister, and now you have to pay."

"Sam, put the knife down and talk to me," Daniel said. He didn't move from his position, as if knowing Sam would see any kind of an advance as a threat.

"There's nothing to talk about," Sam replied. "I see the way you look at her, that happiness that jumps into your eyes. I'll never know that again. Cherry was my only sister, and you took her from me, just like I'm going to take Lizzy from you."

Lizzy felt the prick of the knife tip against her skin, a quick sharp pain and then the warmth of blood. Even when Sam had been beating her she hadn't felt this kind of terror. She also saw a flash of rage in Daniel's eyes, but he remained motionless.

"Sam, I didn't take Cherry away from you. A car accident took her away," Daniel replied, his voice deeper than normal. "And that same accident took away my wife."

"That doesn't matter," Sam replied through clenched teeth. "I don't care about Janice. All I care about is that you never be happy again. And if I kill Lizzy, you'll have the weight of her death forever on her soul."

"Sam, what in the hell are you doing?" Adam Benson stepped through the cabin door.

In the blink of an eye everything changed. As Sam's attention turned toward his brother, he lowered the knife just an inch and loosened his hold on Lizzy. Lizzy flung herself away from him and at the same time Sam pointed his gun at her.

"I don't want to kill you, Sam," Daniel said, his gun pointed at Sam's chest.

"Sam, for God's sake, put down the gun," Adam exclaimed. "What are you doing, man?"

"He took our sister, Adam. He killed her as surely as if he shot her in the heart." Sam's and Daniel's gazes remained locked, the air in the room so tense Lizzy felt as if she might faint. "Now I'm going to take from him."

"Cherry died in a car accident," Adam said, his voice holding a frantic appeal. "You know she always drove too fast. You yelled at her a thousand times about speeding. Sam, Daniel's been our friend since we were kids, and Lizzy has nothing to do with any of it."

"He loves her!" Sam screamed, his hand trembling as it held the gun pointed at Lizzy.

"And I loved Cherry," Daniel replied. His eyes were colder, harder than Lizzy had ever seen them, and she knew then that he would kill his friend to save her life. "She ate at my house, I danced with her at The Corral. We all had drinks together a hundred times. Sam, for God's sake, don't make me shoot you. Put down your gun."

There was a moment when Lizzy thought it was all going to be okay, when the gun in Sam's hand finally swung away from her and she drew in a desperately needed breath of air. But just that quickly it all changed again.

As if in slow motion she saw Sam redirect the gun at her, heard a deafening blast and squeezed her eyes tightly closed. Pain. She waited for it to explode through her as everyone seemed to shout at once.

When she realized she hadn't been shot, she was afraid that if she opened her eyes she'd see Daniel on the floor, dead because he'd made the mistake of loving her. The tremble she'd desperately tried to fight against when the knife blade had been against her throat swooped through her.

"Lizzy." Daniel's voice whispered in her ear, and she didn't have to open her eyes to know that it was his arms that drew her close against his chest. "It's okay now. You're okay."

She gasped in relief and opened her eyes to see Sam on the floor, writhing in pain as he held his bleeding thigh. Sam's gun was in Adam's hand, and Adam looked frozen with shock.

"Nobody move!" Cameron's voice yelled from the doorway. He grabbed the gun from Adam and shoved past him. "What is going on?"

"He shot me!" Sam screamed, in obvious pain. "Get me some medical attention before I bleed to death."

"He tried to kill me, Cameron," Lizzy said, not moving from Daniel's arms. "He's the one who attacked me here before, and in the barn. He was going to kill me and make it look like Candy's murder."

"And I shot him," Daniel said as he tightened his arms around Lizzy.

"She needs to die," Sam shrieked. "I want her dead." He glared at Cameron. "Shoot her. Kill her. He can't have her."

Suddenly the cabin started to fill with people. Daniel pulled Lizzy against a wall as paramedics arrived to load the still-raging Sam. Adam sank down in a nearby chair, his face buried in his hands.

When Sam was gone and Cameron had instructed Deputy Temple to ride with the ambulance, he stood against the wall opposite of Daniel and Lizzy, questions radiating from his eyes. "So, who's ready to talk?"

Lizzy stepped out of Daniel's embrace. "I'll start," she said. "I stepped out of the bathroom and he grabbed me and pulled me into this cabin. Sam is who attacked me the two other times. He just wanted me gone, and when I didn't leave town he decided I needed to die. He wanted to punish Daniel for his sister's death."

"I had to shoot him, Cameron. He was about to shoot Lizzy. I didn't go for a kill shot." Daniel's face was taut with sorrow. "Sam was my friend. I never dreamed he'd do something like this."

Adam raised his head. "He's never been the same since Cherry's death. I told him to get some help, to talk to a therapist or something, but he was just so angry all the time." Adam's dark gaze sought Daniel's. "I'm sorry, man. If I'd known he was really a danger to anyone, I would have done something about it myself."

"You don't owe me any apology," Daniel said.

Adam looked at Lizzy, his eyes filled with misery. "I can't believe he attacked you, that he hurt you so badly before. The man that was in here tonight wasn't my brother. I don't know who that man is."

"He didn't kill Candy," Lizzy said to Cameron. "He told me he didn't, and I believe him. He had a specific reason to come after me. He wanted to punish Daniel, but he had no reason to murder Candy."

Cameron swept a hand across his forehead as if he had the beginnings of a headache. "What I'd like now is for all of us to go down to the office where I can take some official statements."

"What's going to happen to Sam?" Adam asked.

"He'll get the medical treatment he needs and then he'll be arrested for attempted murder," Cameron said, his voice holding the hint of pity for the man.

Adam stood from the chair and straightened his

shoulders. "I'll meet you at the sheriff's office, and in the meantime I've got to get hold of Nick. It's time for him to come home. I can't run that place all by myself."

As he left the room, despite everything that had happened, Lizzy's heart hurt for the man who had not only lost his sister but also, in another way, his brother.

Daniel once again wrapped an arm around Lizzy's shoulders, and as she leaned into him she realized for her it was over. The trembling began all over again as she realized just how very close death had come once again.

"It's over, Lizzy," Daniel said as if he'd read her thoughts. He pulled her into a full embrace and she clung to him. He might have killed a man…a friend, for her. He might have been killed himself in trying to rescue her.

"I'll see you two at the office in a few minutes," Cameron said as he left the cabin.

Lizzy didn't move from Daniel's arms. She had never needed anyone in her life as she needed him then, just to hold her, to assure her with the strength of his arms, the solid beat of his heart, that everything was fine.

"When you didn't come back to the table after going to the bathroom, I sent Mary in to see what was taking so long. When she came back and told me you weren't in there, I panicked." His words whispered against her neck with the heat of emotion. "I was so afraid I'd lost you. I thought I'd made you mad and made you run to danger, just like the night of Janice's death."

She raised her head to look up at him and saw the deep torment in his beautiful gray eyes. "Oh, Daniel, you didn't make me mad. I didn't run out of here angry. I was forced out. I had every intention of coming back to the table to argue with you if I needed to."

His gaze held hers for a long moment. "I don't want to argue with you, Lizzy. I've showed you my hand, my heart, and now the next play is yours." He dropped his arms from around her. "And now we better get down to the sheriff's office and put this terrible night and craziness behind us."

As he led her to his truck, she was vaguely aware of a crowd gathered at the back of the café. But, all she could focus on was what he'd said, that he'd shown her all his cards and now it was her turn to play.

Chapter 13

Lizzy awoke with the late-afternoon sun drifting in through the guest bedroom window at Daniel's place. They hadn't gotten home until just after dawn. It had taken forever at the sheriff's office to finally wrap things up.

Sam had gone through surgery for the gunshot wound to his thigh. Before going in he'd made a full confession to Cameron about the attacks on Lizzy, but he had remained adamant that he'd had nothing to do with Candy's death.

It would take months before a trial, and in the meantime Cameron believed what Sam needed most was some psychological work. Still, he would remain in jail and eventually stand trial for his crimes against Lizzy, the most serious charge one of attempted murder.

She turned over in the bed and stared at the sunbeams dancing across the bottom of the pink comforter, her mind drifting back to the night before. By the time she and Daniel had driven home there had been nothing left to say between them. Both were exhausted, and he'd gone to his room to sleep, and she'd undressed and fallen into bed in this room and slept without dreams.

Daniel had been devastated by Sam's betrayal. Cameron had been upset that he hadn't been able to clear up Candy's murder, and Adam had been distraught to realize how mentally ill his brother had become. Lizzy had felt as if she were on an emotional roller coaster.

It had been a night of high emotions, and by the time it was all over everyone had been wrung dry. Lizzy still felt wrung dry…numb by everything that had happened both before and after Sam had taken her into the cabin.

The conversation she and Daniel had been having before she'd gone to the restroom had been both wonderful and troubling. He loved her. He'd not only said the words out loud, but he'd also shown her through his actions not just last night but also during the past week that they'd spent together.

He'd been a terrific nursemaid while she'd been healing from her beating. He'd anticipated her every need and had been by her side for comfort and support.

Still, she didn't believe his assessment of her, that it was somehow fear that had kept her out of relationships in the past and fear that would take her away from him.

It was just the wrong time in her life for love. She had things to do, places to see and a promise to keep. She got out of bed and headed next door to the bathroom for a hot shower, hoping some clarity would make itself known as she stood beneath a hot spray of water.

By the time she left the bathroom dressed and ready to face the day, she knew the card she was going to play. It took her only fifteen minutes or so to pack her suitcases. She carried them down the stairs and placed them by the front door and then went in search of Daniel.

She found him seated at the kitchen table with a cup of coffee in front of him. Her heart swelled at the sight of him, and she consciously tamped down any emotion that might try to take hold of her.

"You look almost as tired this afternoon as you did this morning when we went to bed," she said to him as she walked over to the coffeepot to pour herself a cup of the fragrant brew.

"Yeah, it took me forever to get to sleep when we got home." He offered her a tired smile as she sat across from him at the table.

"I still can't believe it was Sam who attacked you," he said, his eyes sad as he spoke of the man who had once been his friend. "I never sensed the rage inside him. I never had a clue that he harbored so much resentment against me." He took a sip of his coffee and then smiled at her once again. "But, you look well rested."

"I guess there's nothing quite so good for sleep as knowing the psycho who attacked you is finally behind bars. I slept like a baby."

"Cameron still has his hands full with the investigation into Candy's death."

"He's a smart man. I'm sure he'll have it figured out. Everyone still thinks it's Kevin, and I believe like Cameron does that it's just a matter of time before Kevin tells somebody and the case against him blows wide open."

"I hope so. Somebody needs to pay for that young woman's death." He turned his gaze out the window, and for several long moments an awkward silence prevailed.

She studied his face as he continued to look out the window. She loved the strength that radiated in his features and the softer edge of sensuality that clung to the curve of his mouth.

She loved the way his eyes lit when he smiled, transforming them from a battleship gray to a lighter shade. He had the heart of a warrior, proud and strong, yet protective of the people he loved.

And he loved her.

Her chest tightened as emotion rose up inside her. But, was what he felt for her real love? Could she really depend on that love? Or was it that she'd been the first woman after his tragedy with Janice to come along and he was mistaking his feelings for her?

Maybe he was right about her. Maybe she was just too afraid to trust in any man enough to bind her heart to his. All she really knew was that she needed to leave... and she needed to leave now.

He turned his head and his gaze captured hers, and the sadness in his eyes ached inside her heart, inside her soul. "I heard you carry your suitcases downstairs. I guess that means you've made up your mind to move on."

"Don't look so sad, Daniel," she said, surprised to feel the press of tears at her eyes.

"I am sad, but I think maybe I'm more sad for you

than I am for myself," he replied. "You've opened up my eyes to life again, Lizzy. You've touched my life in such a positive way." His eyes grew darker. "Don't get me wrong. I love you and I don't want you to go. I can't tell you how much it's going to hurt not to have you in my life, but I'm not going to beg you to stay."

Each and every word he spoke cut a gash in her heart that she knew would take a long time to heal. "It's just that I..."

"I know, you have this bucket list thing," he said, interrupting her. "I just hope that when you've finished your bucket list and many adventures and are ready to settle down, you'll find a man who will love you as deeply, as completely as I love you now."

Run. The word flew through her head as tears tumbled from her lashes. "This wasn't supposed to happen," she said, her voice thick with suppressed tears.

"I guess it just proves that you can't dictate when love will enter your life." His gaze held hers for another achingly long moment, and then he abruptly rose from the table and walked over to the sink, where he placed his cup.

She didn't look at him. Run. The word whispered in her head once again. She downed the coffee, the hot liquid burning the back of her throat. She set down her cup and finally got the courage to meet his gaze once again.

"I figured if I left right away I'd be able to get to Kansas City before nightfall."

He nodded, his eyes holding no emotion at all. "Then I guess I'll walk you out."

They said nothing as they reached the front door,

where he picked up her two suitcases as she carried her purse and her cosmetic bag out of the house.

When they reached her car she popped the trunk lid, placed the two suitcases and the makeup bag inside and then closed the lid. When he looked at her again, his eyes brimmed with emotion. Love and sorrow mingled with despair.

He walked with her to her driver door. "I just want to say one last thing," he said before she opened the door to slide into the car.

Please don't, her heart begged. She couldn't take anymore. Her heart was already breaking. She was already torn in half, unsure that the decision she'd made to go was the right one.

"What's that?" she asked with a weary resignation.

"I love you, Lizzy, and I believe we could have something wonderful here together. But, even if you decided to stay, I couldn't make promises to you that we'd never have problems or that I wouldn't sometimes let you down or disappoint you. Of course, I'd do everything in my power not to do those things, but I need you to know that I'm not like your father."

He reached out and softly touched her cheek. "I would never be that man in your life. I would never leave you sitting all alone on a stoop waiting for me, whether you were my wife or my child."

At that moment his heart was so open, so vulnerable to her, that it was painful to see and know that she was going to turn her back and run from Grady Gulch, from him and from love.

Right man, wrong time, she told herself as she murmured a quick, choked goodbye. Reluctantly he stepped away from her door and she started the engine.

She pulled away from his house without looking back in her mirror. She didn't want to catch one last glimpse of him. She didn't want the last look she had of him to be in her rearview mirror as she drove away from what he was offering her.

She just wanted to be on the road, footloose and fancy-free as she'd intended when she'd first arrived in Grady Gulch.

She emptied her mind, numb as minutes later she drove past the Cowboy Café and all the people she'd come to love who worked there.

She didn't stop. Her heart couldn't stand another goodbye. She just wanted to drive with the window down and the breeze blowing every thought of Grady Gulch and Daniel Jefferson out of her mind.

The numbness lasted until she was about forty miles away from Grady Gulch, and then the emotions she'd tried so hard to control exploded wildly. She pulled the car to the side of the road as tears blinded her vision.

Dropping her head to the steering wheel, she wept because she really didn't want to go forward, but she was too afraid to go back.

It had been almost three hours since Lizzy had left, and Daniel's heart had never felt heavier, the house had never seemed so empty.

He'd done what he could to make her stay. He'd filleted his heart on a stone before her, but she'd chosen her bucket list over him. There had been nothing more he could do.

She'd been a temporary gift in his life, an awakening that he'd desperately needed, and now she was gone and his heartache was almost unbearable.

But, instead of the weight of guilt and heartache that had kept him housebound and isolated before Lizzy came to town, he felt the need to surround himself with people and noise.

He grabbed his hat and car keys and headed for his truck and the Cowboy Café, where he knew he'd find food and noise and good friends and neighbors.

As deeply as his heart ached with the loss of Lizzy, he no longer believed he was a man who was meant to be alone, who deserved to be alone and miserable.

Eventually he would find his life partner, the soul mate who would help him fill his big house with children, who would stand beside him through the hard times and celebrate with him the good ones.

He'd wanted that woman to be Lizzy. He'd believed her to be Lizzy, and right now he couldn't imagine the woman in his life being anyone else but Lizzy.

He pulled into the café parking lot. As usual it was a fairly full house, and he suspected he and Sam and the drama last night with Lizzy was probably the hottest topic of conversation.

He entered the café, and as he hung his hat on one of the hooks, he glanced toward the counter. A piercing ache resounded in him as he saw Mary, not Lizzy, standing there. He made his way to a stool and sat.

"Where's your better half?" Mary asked.

"She left town a couple of hours ago."

"Without saying goodbye?" Mary asked with obvious disappointment.

"I think saying goodbye would have been too hard on her." Daniel heard the hollow ring in his voice.

"I'm so sorry, Daniel," Mary said as if she knew his heartache.

"Yeah, so am I." He drew a deep sigh. "She never lied about her plans. From the very first she met me, she told me that this was just a temporary stop along her way. We all just borrowed her for a little while, but she was never really ours to keep." The words shot another layer of pain through his heart.

He felt a small edge of relief as the conversation turned to the events of the night before. It still felt like a strange dream…the cabin and Sam and Lizzy.

He'd never forget that moment when Sam's knife had pricked the tender skin on Lizzy's neck and blood had appeared. If he hadn't been afraid of hitting Lizzy, Daniel would have shot Sam then and there, and he wouldn't have aimed for his leg.

It would have hurt him, to shoot a man who had been his friend since childhood, but Adam was right when he'd said that man in the cabin the night before hadn't been the real Sam. The real Sam had been lost to grief when his sister died.

The night of that accident, grief and guilt had transformed Daniel into an isolated, self-punishing man, and apparently that same accident had turned Sam into a seething monster wanting revenge. As long as Daniel had remained a miserable soul, the monster had been satisfied. But when Lizzy had entered Daniel's life and transformed it, Sam's seething need for revenge, his desire to see Daniel miserable forever, had exploded.

He gave Mary his dinner order and then found himself inundated with people stopping by his stool to find out all the details of what had happened the night before and to offer their support.

He realized how much people cared about Lizzy and about him, and he was reminded once again about the things he loved about Grady Gulch. This was his home and, even though he knew it would take months before the loss of Lizzy stopped piercing his heart, at least he had friends and the Cowboy Café to ease some of that pain.

He was halfway through his meal when he smelled her, that slightly exotic fragrance that always tightened his muscles with desire. For a moment he thought he was fantasizing it, that his grief over the loss of her was playing games with his senses. Then she was there, standing next to him, that bright, beautiful smile curving her lips. His heart nearly jumped out of his chest.

"Mind if I sit here, cowboy?" she asked as she slid onto the stool next to his.

"Don't mind a bit," he replied and scooted the small plate with a slice of apple pie on it that he had ordered in front of her.

She gasped in surprise. "You were expecting me?"

His heart had accelerated in pace the moment he'd smelled the scent of her, the moment he'd turned to see her standing next to him. "Not exactly expecting you. I just couldn't let go of a little bit of hope. So, tell me,

Elizabeth Wiles but everybody calls you Lizzy, how you happen to be in Grady Gulch eating my piece of apple pie?"

"A funny thing happened on the way to my bucket list." She picked up a fork and took a bite of the pie and then continued. "I got an hour out of town, and with each mile that passed I kept thinking about everything you'd said to me and all that I was leaving behind."

She set the fork down and turned in the stool as he did the same, her knees coming to stop between his. "You were right about everything, Daniel. I was afraid. I was willing to climb a mountain all by myself, to wander the streets of New York City alone, but I was absolutely terrified to reach out and grab on to the love you offered me."

All the clatter of the diners in the café fell away, all the talking and noise completely disappeared as Daniel focused solely on the woman in front of him. At that moment it was as if the two of them were completely alone. All that mattered was her.

"Anyway, I finally pulled to the side of the road and started to cry." Those beautiful whiskey-colored eyes of hers held his gaze intently. "I thought about the bucket list and I thought about you, and then I thought about my mother and what she would have wanted for me."

He couldn't stand it any longer. He had to touch her in some way. He reached for her hand, and she took it and squeezed as if she never wanted to let it go.

"I think Mom's goal with wanting me to do the bucket list was really a ruse to make me stop and take stock of the life I was leading when she died. She worried about me having nothing but work in my life, worried that I was getting closer and closer to thirty and didn't have any hint of a meaningful relationship with anyone. I know now exactly what Mom wanted for me, and it wasn't singing on a corner in Times Square. It's you, Daniel."

"That's nice, but I need to hear what *you* want, what you need," he replied. He'd waited for what felt like a lifetime for the words to come from her, the words he'd longed to hear.

The light that shone from her eyes was near-blinding and he fell into the flames, loving her so much he wondered how he'd lived a day of his life without her.

"I love you, Daniel, and I'm not afraid anymore. I trust in our love. I need you. I want to share your life with you, fill that house with babies and be with you to watch our grandchildren play in the yard."

For a moment he couldn't speak. His chest was so filled with his heart it held the air in his lungs captive. He released her hand and stood and then pulled her up and into his arms, and their lips met in a kiss that tasted of cinnamon and apples, of passion and laughter and, most of all, love.

The people in the café cheered, and as the kiss finally ended Lizzy looked up at Daniel and smiled. "I'm home, Daniel. I'm finally truly home."

Epilogue

Mary Mathis gasped for air and sat up, her heart pounding a thousand beats a minute. Anxiety pressed tight in her chest, a familiar but unwanted enemy.

Telling herself to relax, to breathe in and out in slow, measured breaths, she felt her heart slowing to a more normal pace, the sickening anxiety beginning to fade.

When would these episodes fade? When would the dreams of the past finally leave her alone? Allow her to sleep and stop worrying?

She got out of bed and as always went to the doorway of Matt's bedroom, comforted by the sight of him sleeping soundly. She returned to the living room, turned on the end table lamp and curled up on the sofa.

It had been almost a month since Candy's death and still nobody was in jail for the crime, and Mary couldn't stop the faint niggling feeling that something else bad was coming.

She'd dismiss it as nothing more than a foolish woman's intuition, but at one time years ago Mary had been quite adept at forecasting danger. She'd been able to feel it in the air, taste it in the terror that welled up in the back of her throat.

She felt that now, but this time the terror didn't have a name, it didn't have a face, and that scared her as much as anything.

Think about something positive, she commanded herself as she pulled an afghan from the back of the sofa and covered her bare legs.

She'd managed to hire a new waitress, a young woman named Lynette Shiver, who was taking Lizzy's place and had the same kind of bright, cheerful personality.

A smile curved Mary's lips as she thought of Lizzy. Although she missed her working in the café, it had been wonderful watching Daniel and Lizzy's love grow stronger every day. They came into the café twice a week for dinner, and it was obvious a wedding was in the near future.

A wave of loneliness struck Mary. Most of the time she stayed too busy to miss the presence of a male in her life. She had her work at the café and Matt to keep her busy, but there were moments when she longed for something she could never have, for somebody to wrap her in his strong arms and talk to her of love.

But, the actions she'd taken years ago, the decisions she'd made for herself and for Matt, made it impossible for her to invite a man in, especially the man who looked at her with desire.

Sheriff Cameron Evans had made it clear in a million ways that he was interested in her. But, even though the sight of him created a warm pool of desire inside her, even though she admired him more than anyone else she'd ever met in her life, he was off-limits now and forever.

A shiver whispered through her, and it had nothing to do with her thoughts of Cameron Evans. Rather, it was the feeling that evil had come to Grady Gulch, and it wasn't about to move on any time soon.

* * * * *

**COMING NEXT MONTH from Harlequin®
Romantic Suspense**
AVAILABLE JULY 24, 2012

#1715 CAVANAUGH RULES
Cavanaugh Justice
Marie Ferrarella
Two emotionally closed-off homicide detectives take a chance on love while working a case together.

#1716 BREATHLESS ENCOUNTER
Code X
Cindy Dees
A genetically enhanced hero on a mission to draw out modern-day pirates rescues the woman who may actually be their target.

#1717 THE REUNION MISSION
Black Ops Rescues
Beth Cornelison
A black ops soldier and the woman who once betrayed him confront their undeniable attraction while he guards her and a vulnerable child in a bayou hideaway.

#1718 SEDUCING THE COLONEL'S DAUGHTER
All McQueen's Men
Jennifer Morey
It's this operative's mission to bring a kidnapped woman home. Will the headstrong daughter of a powerful colonel take his heart when he does?

You can find more information on upcoming Harlequin®
titles, free excerpts and more at www.Harlequin.com.

HRSCNM0712

REQUEST YOUR FREE BOOKS!
2 FREE NOVELS PLUS 2 FREE GIFTS!

ROMANTIC
SUSPENSE
Sparked by Danger, Fueled by Passion.

YES! Please send me 2 FREE Harlequin® Romantic Suspense novels and my 2 FREE gifts (gifts are worth about $10). After receiving them, if I don't wish to receive any more books, I can return the shipping statement marked "cancel." If I don't cancel, I will receive 4 brand-new novels every month and be billed just $4.49 per book in the U.S. or $5.24 per book in Canada. That's a saving of at least 14% off the cover price! It's quite a bargain! Shipping and handling is just 50¢ per book in the U.S. and 75¢ per book in Canada.* I understand that accepting the 2 free books and gifts places me under no obligation to buy anything. I can always return a shipment and cancel at any time. Even if I never buy another book, the two free books and gifts are mine to keep forever.

240/340 HDN FEFR

Name	(PLEASE PRINT)	
Address		Apt. #
City	State/Prov.	Zip/Postal Code

Signature (if under 18, a parent or guardian must sign)

Mail to the **Reader Service:**
IN U.S.A.: P.O. Box 1867, Buffalo, NY 14240-1867
IN CANADA: P.O. Box 609, Fort Erie, Ontario L2A 5X3

Not valid for current subscribers to Harlequin Romantic Suspense books.

Want to try two free books from another line?
Call 1-800-873-8635 or visit www.ReaderService.com.

* Terms and prices subject to change without notice. Prices do not include applicable taxes. Sales tax applicable in N.Y. Canadian residents will be charged applicable taxes. Offer not valid in Quebec. This offer is limited to one order per household. All orders subject to credit approval. Credit or debit balances in a customer's account(s) may be offset by any other outstanding balance owed by or to the customer. Please allow 4 to 6 weeks for delivery. Offer available while quantities last.

Your Privacy—The Reader Service is committed to protecting your privacy. Our Privacy Policy is available online at www.ReaderService.com or upon request from the Reader Service.

We make a portion of our mailing list available to reputable third parties that offer products we believe may interest you. If you prefer that we not exchange your name with third parties, or if you wish to clarify or modify your communication preferences, please visit us at www.ReaderService.com/consumerschoice or write to us at Reader Service Preference Service, P.O. Box 9062, Buffalo, NY 14269. Include your complete name and address.

HRS11B

Werewolf and elite U.S. Navy SEAL, Matt Parker, must set aside his prejudices and partner with beautiful Fae Sienna McClare to find a magic orb that threatens to expose the secret nature of his entire team.

Harlequin® Nocturne presents the debut of beloved author Bonnie Vanak's new miniseries, PHOENIX FORCE.

Enjoy a sneak preview of THE COVERT WOLF, available August 2012 from Harlequin® Nocturne.

Sienna McClare was Fae, accustomed to open air and fields. Not this boxy subway car.

As the oily smell of fear clogged her nostrils, she inhaled deeply, tried thinking of tall pines waving in the wind, the chatter of birds and a deer cropping grass. A wolf watching a deer, waiting. Prey. Images of fangs flashing, tearing, wet sounds…

No!

She fought the panic freezing her blood. And was gradually able to push the fear down into a dark spot deep inside her. The stench of Draicon werewolf clung to her like cheap perfume.

Sienna hated glamouring herself as a Draicon werewolf, but it was necessary if she was going to find the Orb of Light. Someone had stolen the Orb from her colony, the Los Lobos Fae. A Draicon who'd previously been seen in the area was suspected. Sienna had eagerly seized the chance to help when asked because finding it meant she would no longer be an outcast. The Fae had cast her out when she turned twenty-one because she was the bastard child of a sweet-faced Fae and a Draicon killer. But if she found the Orb, Sienna could return to the only home she'd known. It also meant she could recover her lost memories.

Every time she tried searching for her past, she met with a closed door. Who was she? Which side ruled her?

Fae or Draicon?

Draicon, no way in hell.

Sensing someone staring, she glanced up, saw a man across the aisle. He was heavily muscled and radiated power and confidence. Yet he also had the face of a gentle warrior. Sienna's breath caught. She felt a stir of sexual chemistry.

He was as lonely and grief stricken as she was. Her heart twisted. Who had hurt this man? She wanted to go to him, comfort him and ease his sorrow. Sienna smiled.

An odd connection flared between them. Sienna locked her gaze to his, desperately needing someone who understood.

Then her nostrils flared as she caught his scent. Hatred boiled to the surface. Not a man. Draicon.

The enemy.

Find out what happens next in THE COVERT WOLF by Bonnie Vanak.

Available August 2012 from Harlequin® Nocturne wherever books are sold.